"I neve pulled back in."

She felt that statement to her very core.

"I don't know what you want me to say," Erin admitted honestly. "We both have different lives. I'm here, you're there. Nothing has changed in ten years except now you're a father and I'm a foster mom."

That muscle ticked in his jaw again as if frustration had settled in.

"How is this even possible?" she added. "So much time and distance between us and yet, there's still something."

Joe's other hand came up and framed her face as that penetrating stare held her in place. He had the most gentle touch for someone with such a commanding presence. He'd always been a tender leader.

She just wished he hadn't been called to lead so far away. But wishes wouldn't change the past or the present.

Julia Ruth is a *USA TODAY* bestselling author. She is married to her high school sweetheart and values her faith and family above all else. Julia and her husband have two teen girls and they enjoy their beach trips, where they can unwind and get back to basics. Since she grew up in a small rural community, Julia loves keeping her settings in fictitious towns that make her readers feel like they're home. You can find Julia on Instagram at juliaruthbooks.

Books by Julia Ruth

Love Inspired

Four Sisters Ranch

A Cowgirl's Homecoming
The Cowboy's Inheritance
The Sheriff Next Door
Reuniting with the Cowboy

Visit the Author Profile page at LoveInspired.com.

REUNITING WITH THE COWBOY

JULIA RUTH

LOVE INSPIRED
INSPIRATIONAL ROMANCE

LOVE INSPIRED®
INSPIRATIONAL ROMANCE

ISBN-13: 978-1-335-62104-7

Reuniting with the Cowboy

Recycling programs
for this product may
not exist in your area.

Love Inspired
22 Adelaide St. West, 41st Floor
Toronto, Ontario M5H 4E3, Canada
www.LoveInspired.com

Printed in Lithuania

MIX
Paper | Supporting
responsible forestry
FSC® C021394

In all thy ways acknowledge him,
and he shall direct thy paths.
—*Proverbs* 3:6

To anyone who is afraid to take that leap of faith
and try again...do it.

This is your time!

Chapter One

Erin Spencer clutched the basket of jams and produce leftover from the farmer's market in one hand and held on to the hand of her foster child in the other. In the two days she'd been with Willow, Erin had come to realize the child needed comfort and nurturing more than anything. Holding hands seemed to help Willow cope, but Erin still couldn't get the six-year-old to say much. A few one- or two-word sentences here and there was about all.

One hurdle at a time.

Erin mounted the steps to Garnet Trulane's two-story yellow cottage. At one time the elderly woman held a special place in Erin's life. Garnet's grandson had been "the one"…or so Erin had thought. But since he left nearly ten years ago, Garnet and Erin's strained relationship had gone nowhere.

Yet here Erin stood with baked goods and jarred jams in hand because she was the only Spencer family member available this morning for a delivery.

Her mother, Sarah Spencer, baked and canned year-round, keeping Rosewood Valley's pantries well-stocked—including, and especially, Garnet Trulane's. Her family often sent food to the elderly woman, and usually Erin's job as a teacher often prevented her from being the one to deliver. Today, not so. Just because Erin and Garnet had a wedge between them didn't mean Sarah and Garnet did. The two women were rather close.

"Would you like to ring the doorbell?" Erin asked Willow.

Willow's wide brown eyes came up to meet Erin's. The little girl wore a brand-new yellow ribbon in her dark curly hair. Erin gestured toward the round button on the white door frame.

"Go ahead," she encouraged.

Willow released Erin's hand and reached for the doorbell. The delicate chime echoed from inside the home and onto the covered porch. Erin waited as thoughts rolled through her mind of all she needed to get done today. Thankfully she was on summer break and could devote herself to this critical time with Willow, but she could also help more at Four Sisters Ranch with her family. The new space for their farm-to-table events had really taken off over the last year and she could offer more of her time now. Well, that had been her intention before Willow, but perhaps Willow could come with her and it would help her to feel part of the family as well. Anything to help this sweet girl become more engaged and feel loved and wanted.

The door opened and Erin had about a half second to process her past standing before her.

"Erin?"

Wearing a simple white T-shirt and dark jeans, Joe Trulane seemed just as surprised to see Erin as she was to see him. About a month ago Garnet had been all too eager to tell Erin of Joe's upcoming return, but the exact date had been a mystery.

The mystery was no more. The man she'd always thought she'd marry stood before her looking just as handsome with that familiar crooked grin and those bright blue eyes.

Yet the soft lines around his mouth and along his forehead were new and there was a hint of emotion staring back at her she couldn't quite put her finger on.

"I heard you were coming back." Erin offered a smile, hoping to push beyond the awkward nerves and ribbon of anxiety in her belly. "I'm just dropping off some of my mother's goodies for Garnet."

She held up the basket just as a little girl ran up to Joe and slammed into the side of his leg. Erin's breath caught in her throat as her chest tightened. Everything she'd ever wanted stood right here in this circle. A family with Joe, a simple life, a farm, a home to call their own. She didn't think she'd asked for too much, but when they'd laid out their future, she'd learned he hadn't wanted children. Then he'd been called away for his dream mission work. How could she argue or try to persuade him to stay at that point?

After Joe left, Erin had tried dating. She'd even thought herself serious about one guy, but something had always been missing. Even though she'd been young and in love with Joe, she quickly learned her feelings for him had been true and genuine. Age hadn't mattered one bit.

"Daddy, I thought we were having ice-cream sundaes?" the little girl said, staring up at Joe, clearly more concerned about her ice cream and not the visitors.

Daddy.

Who knew one simple word could be so gut-wrenching? She'd always assumed they shared the same goals…then Joe got called into mission work and was gone. Maybe she'd been so blind with love and her own dreams she'd completely missed his.

At least now she knew a little more about his life, but she'd be lying if she didn't admit the sting knowing he'd found her dream with someone else brought on a new layer of pain she hadn't anticipated.

Joe glanced from the little girl back to Erin and chuckled.

"Don't judge me for giving her ice cream for breakfast," he said. "It's our thing. Just a little treat once every so often and I figured coming home was a special occasion."

Yes, coming home was a special occasion, and clearly she wasn't coping with the shock of seeing him in person again. That needed to change and fast. She could push aside memories of the last time they both stood on this porch crying and saying goodbye.

"No judgment here," Erin confirmed. "I love ice cream for breakfast." Erin turned her attention to the little girl with a pink headband holding back her long curly hair. "My name is Erin. What's your name?"

She looked to Erin but rested her cheek against Joe's leg. "Ada."

Erin grinned. "Well, Ada, how old are you?"

"Seven."

Oh, the irony cut deep. As if seeing Joe wasn't enough of a heartache, knowing his daughter was nearly the same age as Erin's foster really just seemed like a smack in the face. But she firmly believed everything happened for a reason… She just always wished she knew what those reasons were. Why had he decided after he'd gone away that he wanted a family? He'd left at eighteen, determined to dedicate his life to missionary work. In particular, Joe had cited not wanting to settle down too soon as the reason for their breakup. He was young and felt called to accomplish a whole list of things first. Yet a few years later at twenty-one, he'd become a dad? Had he just not wanted children and a life with her?

"This is Willow." Erin slid her arm around Willow's shoulders to make her daughter feel more secure and to have a source of stability for herself. "She's six, but she's a little bit shy around new people."

Joe studied Willow before his gaze moved back to Erin. "Ada could talk enough for both of them." He chuckled.

Ada smiled. "I do like to talk. Sometimes I get in trouble in class, but I can't help it. I just have all these ideas and if I keep everything inside, I might forget all of them."

Oh, she was precious and reminded Erin so much of the kids in her class. Erin wanted to know more about Joe's time away, where his wife was or if she'd traveled back from Africa with him. Clearly he'd made the life he'd wanted. Strange, Garnet had never mentioned Joe having a family. Erin wasn't close to her anymore, but surely the woman would've told her mother. And Sarah would've told her. She'd have to ask her mother about it.

"I bet Willow would like ice cream," Joe muttered toward Ada. "What do you think?"

Erin stilled. She couldn't stay. She *shouldn't* stay. Her mind was still processing way too much and to enter this house and try to act like the inner turmoil didn't exist was simply absurd. Not to mention she and Garnet had barely spoken but just a few times since Joe left years ago and one of those times was just a month ago when Garnet was all too thrilled to announce Joe's upcoming return.

But that little tug on her hand pulled Erin from her worrisome thoughts.

She glanced down at Willow and the wide eyes staring back at her as she gave a little nod.

How could Erin say no when Willow hadn't asked for one thing and hadn't expressed much since being removed from her home?

Erin looked back to Joe and suppressed a sigh. Looked like she was about to face her past whether she was ready or not.

What had he been thinking? Inviting Erin into his grandmother's home like they were old classmates who'd run into each other and were catching up. Maybe if he pretended they were just old friends, the threat of anything awkward would be eliminated.

Joe couldn't think about their last encounter, not without revisiting the pain he'd caused her. The image of one tear after another sliding down her cheeks as she tried to smile and wish him the best as he went off to do God's will. She'd selflessly let him go and he'd watched as her heart broke, which only broke his own heart even more. He'd been so torn and prayed over his decision, but he couldn't ignore his calling, just as she hadn't been able to ignore her own. Their life goals had been too opposite, something the teens in love hadn't discussed until he'd been given the opportunity to leave town and he'd accepted…assuming she'd follow.

But Erin had wanted the small-town married life with kids, and he'd wanted to save the world.

So they'd gone in opposite directions down different paths…yet somehow managed to land right back here. Both of them had children now—which hadn't been in his plans at all. But the tragic passing of his friends, also missionaries, had led to his adopting Ada. And that had been a blessing.

He wanted to know more about Erin's little girl and the life she led, but he couldn't jump in with that. Granted, his Gram was all too eager to fill him in on what Erin had been up to over this past decade. He'd heard when she got a job teaching—which hadn't surprised him as she was great with kids. He'd heard when she'd moved off the ranch and into a small cottage in town. Gram had even kept Joe informed as to whom Erin had dated over the years. He'd tried to shut that information out, never examining too closely why it should bother him. Somehow his Gram failed to mention Erin had a child, but all of Gram's information came secondhand from church or Erin's mother.

Joe stepped inside and out of the way, allowing Erin and Willow to enter. He immediately remembered his manners, which had temporarily vanished at the shock of his morning visitor.

He gestured to the basket. "Let me take that."

Without thinking, he reached out the same time she moved forward. His hand brushed hers and he froze. Her eyes darted up to his.

Well, well, well. It seemed neither of them were immune to this reunion. That should really be no surprise, considering the past they shared. But did that bond still span two continents and an entire decade?

Seeing as they both had a little audience, anything he would want to bring up would have to wait. Joe wouldn't even know what to say, anyway.

"I'll take it," he offered again.

Erin quickly let go and Joe didn't miss the way she took a step back. She had always been one to control her emotions and keep a peaceful atmosphere.

"Is Garnet home?" Erin asked, glancing from the foyer toward the living room.

"She ran to the feedstore to grab some ferns for the ladies' luncheon at church this Saturday. Should be back soon."

"Come on into the kitchen," Ada chimed in, extending her hand toward Willow. "I'll show you where the ice cream is and you can pick your toppings. Dad bought all the good stuff."

Willow froze, her eyes wide as she looked to Erin. Joe recognized the fear and wondered what had happened in her short life to make her so hesitant to go with another child for a sweet treat. This was the most innocent moment, yet the little girl didn't move. The juxtaposition between the two girls wasn't lost on him, yet Ada never met a stranger she didn't like. Considering he didn't know Willow, he wasn't sure if this was a good or bad encounter.

"I'm coming," Erin assured Willow. "You can go and I promise I'll be right there."

Willow slowly reached for Ada's hand and the biggest smile spread across Ada's face. Joe had wondered if she would meet any friends around her age during this summer visit. He assumed she'd find someone in class at Sunday school. Never in his wildest dreams had he thought Ada's first buddy would be the daughter of his high school sweetheart. He knew he'd have to find Ada some type of summer school or tutoring so she could get caught up before they went back to Senegal. Her learning skills weren't quite up to her age, so he'd assumed she'd find friends down that avenue. She could speak French and English fluently, as both were spoken in their town, but the written English portion of her studies and the cognitive side of learning had been more of a struggle than Joe thought.

The moment the girls started down the hallway, Joe focused his attention back on Erin. She, however, kept her gaze over his shoulder. Those familiar green eyes hadn't changed. They were still vibrant, beautiful and so striking he could easily get lost once again in them. She obviously still had her long silky blond hair, but it was all twisted up in a knot on top of her head. A few wayward strands framed her delicate face. She hadn't changed a bit. That sweet girl-next-door appeal still held so much weight. He hadn't expected just how much.

But he wasn't some teen concerned about taking a pretty girl to the homecoming dance. No, he had much bigger issues now and someone else to think about other than himself, Anything they had in the past, and any attraction he felt for her now, had to remain there.

"I feel like we're intruding," Erin told him.

Joe shook his head. "Absolutely not. No matter what happened or how you and Gram are now, she would still want me to remember my manners."

Erin blinked her emerald eyes his direction and smiled. "She always insists I come in for tea. Mom talked about Willow and I was actually hoping Garnet could meet her today."

Meet Willow? Wasn't she Erin's daughter, and wouldn't Garnet have been introduced by now?

"They've never met?" Joe asked, knowing full well none of this was his concern or business.

Erin tucked a strand of blond hair behind her ear and pursed her lips. "It's a long story, but no. They haven't met."

Interesting. Had the wedge between Garnet and Erin been that wide that his Gram hadn't met Erin's daughter?

Or…maybe this was one of her sister's children. He hadn't kept up with her three other sisters so he really had no idea where their lives had taken them. Joe suddenly found he wanted to uncover everything…another time and under other circumstances perhaps.

She glanced down the hall again. "I should get in there."

Erin started to ease by him in the narrow foyer and he couldn't ignore that sweet floral aroma that enveloped him.

The ringing of a cell phone stopped her and she reached into the pocket of her long skirt and pulled out her cell.

She swiped her finger across the screen and answered. "Hello."

He didn't want to listen in so he sauntered away, pulling out his own phone and checking his email. There in his inbox was a new one from the mission he worked with in Senegal—as if he needed the reminder that there were some important decisions to make in the very near future.

And reminding him how he was very much caught between two places.

Did he stay and try to build a life here in Rosewood Valley? His Gram would love nothing more than to get to know his daughter and had said so many times. Added to that, Ada's parents were also originally from California. They were both killed just weeks after Ada's birth and the only living relative Ada had left was her biological maternal grandmother, still in Cali. In just a short time they would have their first face-to-face meeting. With both grandmothers being elderly, traveling alone was a bit too much and with Joe's heavy mission load, making a trip home hadn't been possible before now. But Joe had always kept them in video and text contact because he knew the importance of family...which was why this crossroads in his life was so difficult.

He'd basically been handed his dream mission field position, the one he'd worked for over the past decade. How could he turn down the offer he'd been given to start up his own mission group in Western Africa and be the sole leader?

But Ada's learning disabilities over the past couple years had left her behind the other children her age, and he couldn't help but wonder if she'd get a better education here. He truly didn't know, but taking this summer to visit Gram and pray over this next step was all he could do. The constant volley back and forth in his mind over the pros and cons of each decision never ended.

"Is the decision final?"

Erin's words, with the fear lacing her tone, pulled him from his own thoughts.

"No." She closed her eyes as she rubbed her forehead. "I can come clean my room out myself… I'm just blind-sided, that's all."

Blindsided.

Her voice cracked and Joe started to take a step forward, but he didn't know what she was dealing with or if she even wanted comfort. His gut tightened seeing Erin so broken up about whatever had just happened. She'd always been so strong and right now she looked lost.

But that was the Erin he knew ten years ago. He didn't know this version of Erin.

When she disconnected the call, she turned her back to him and pulled in a shaky breath. He wasn't sure what to say. Over the years he'd ministered to thousands and always managed to find the right words or at least offer a source of strength during a difficult time.

Yet he and Erin had a unique relationship and he stood on shaky ground so he had to wait, allowing her to take the lead. He also didn't want to ask the obvious question of if everything was okay because clearly a part of her world had just crumbled. He respected her enough to give her time to gather herself so she could hold on to her pride.

Just like the Erin he recalled, she squared her shoulders and turned back to face him. Though her eyes were damp with unshed tears, she tipped her chin as if adamant about appearing strong.

"I need to get Willow and go," she informed him. "I just found out I lost my job so I need to go clean my classroom."

She made the statement almost matter-of-factly. Her brow was creasing a little, though, which was a big indicator of her worry and confusion.

Joe knew she was a teacher through his Gram, but he couldn't fathom why she'd lose her job. They'd lost touch for a decade, but he hadn't met many people who adored children more than Erin... That had been their ultimate bone of contention in the end. Their life and timeline goals simply hadn't lined up and high school love couldn't carry them through reality.

She shrugged. "Apparently there were budget cuts and they had to let three teachers go," she went on with a slight sniff. "I was one of the unlucky ones. I just didn't see this coming. I knew of budget issues, but didn't know they were bad enough for layoffs."

She closed her eyes and shook her head as she whispered, "I don't know what this will mean for my foster care."

Foster care. So that was why Gram hadn't met Willow. If Erin couldn't work, would the system take Willow away? Most likely...which would just be another devastating blow to Erin and who knew how another drastic change would affect Willow.

Joe didn't think before speaking or acting. He closed the distance between them and placed his hands on her delicate shoulders. As those deep green eyes came up to meet his, Joe's gut tightened with worry and a punch of attraction he hadn't experienced in quite some time.

"I'll make sure Willow stays where she is," he assured her. "I need a tutor for Ada and you're the perfect person."

She looked confused. "A tutor? But I can't..."

"You need to stay employed, right?"

Erin nodded, her gaze never wavering.

"Well I need one-on-one aid for my girl. At least for the summer." Joe stepped back and extended his hand. "Do we have a deal?"

Erin's gaze dropped down, and for a second he thought she might deny him, but ultimately she reached for him. Her palm slid into his and she gripped his hand as she shook and nodded.

"Deal."

Chapter Two

"Willow, could you take this box over to that bookshelf in the corner and try to fit as many books as you can inside?"

Erin never thought she'd be packing up the cozy little schoolroom she'd taken so much time and care to decorate. Yet here she was. She'd left Garnet's house before Joe's Gram had returned—Erin wasn't sure if that was a blessing or not.

Between the bombshell of the job loss, seeing Joe and then making a commitment to tutor his daughter, Erin's nerves were shot.

Once Willow had finished her sundae, Erin had stopped at the feedstore owned by her new brother-in-law and sister and grabbed some empty boxes. Thankfully neither had seen her. Erin had snuck in the back, taken just a few from the storage room, and left. She didn't want to answer questions now, not when her emotions were too raw. The hits had come all morning from a variety of angles and she needed some time to regroup and refocus.

Willow took the box and made her way to the other side of the bright, cheery room. Erin had taught for about six years and had gone between first and second grade, depending on the size of the classes and the need for an extra teacher. She loved nothing more than helping young minds grow and she couldn't imagine not returning in the fall. Not starting at the first of August, making individual name cards, and labeling all the cubbies and bins. Her gaze roamed over the empty desks and images of all the kids she'd taught over the years filled her mind.

That familiar burn in her throat as her eyes welled up with tears was both unwanted and unnecessary. She didn't have time for the tears or any type of self-pity party. She needed to get this room cleaned out and focus on Willow. Right now Willow had to be her top priority. That sweet girl had been through so much already in her six short years. With her mother having passed away and her addicted father, her home life had been nothing short of unsettling and tragic.

Providing a stable environment full of love and faith was what Willow needed. Erin had to lean in on that faith right now, praying God had something even better for her behind another door rather than the one that had just closed in her face.

Erin forced herself to focus. She couldn't get this done just standing around letting years of memories play out before her. There was no way she could get this entire room cleaned out in one trip, but thankfully she had done quite a bit already at the end of the school year. There was still so much personal stuff that she always kept in her room, though. The seasonal decorations and learning games, the special rugs for designated playtime, all the little touches she'd always had so she could make her room feel cozy and interactive for each student. This classroom would likely be used for something else, so it'd all have to go.

She decided to start with her desk where her most important things were. Erin sat a box on her swivel chair and glanced to the variety of the photos on her bulletin board behind her computer monitor. Over the years her kids would bring in school pictures and she would proudly display each one. There was no way she could toss those. Her students were just like her own family.

Erin grabbed the desk organizer with her notecards, pens and clips, and sat the entire unit in the box. Then she turned to get the photos in frames from her desk and carefully placed each one down in the box.

"Ooh!"

Willow's gasp of delight had Erin's attention moving across the room. The little girl had her eyes glued to one of the books Erin always read her class. The adorable short story with farm animals all talking to each other and helping one another was so uplifting and she tried to instill that selfless attitude in each of her students

"Do you like that one?" Erin asked.

Willow nodded, her dark eyes still on the cover.

"You can have it," Erin offered. "Set that one aside so we don't lose it. We can read it before bedtime tonight. Sound like a plan?"

A wide smile spread across Willow's face and she nodded as she sat the book on the closest desk. In the very short time they had been together, Erin hadn't heard many words out of Willow's mouth and she'd shown very little emotion. But the ice cream and the book, those were things Erin could work with. Slow progress was at least progress.

A few days ago, when Erin had gotten the call that a foster was ready, there hadn't been time for anything other than getting in the car and going to the children's services office. Erin had stepped in to see the sweetest little face and the little girl only had a small plastic bag of her belongings beside her. That was all. Just one tiny grocery store–sized bag. There had been one mismatched outfit, one stuffed unicorn, and one tattered book. Erin's heart had broken immediately and the moment they'd left, Erin took Willow and let her pick out a couple new outfits, some pajamas, and another pair of shoes. She'd turned down another toy or anything else. Poor thing was likely used to getting nothing and Erin didn't want to overload her, but Willow clearly needed necessities and she also needed toys and books to live her life as a healthy child should.

Erin had wanted to be a mother for as long as she could remember; she'd had the best role model, after all. She thought by this age she'd already have a husband and children, but no. She'd dated since Joe left, but nobody matched her. Going into education had opened her eyes to the need to love on children who felt no love, no stability. Fostering seemed like the perfect road to take to spread the love of God and fulfill her desires to be a mother.

A tap on the door frame pulled Erin's attention from the heartbreaking scene from just days ago to the opening of her classroom where her eldest sister, Rachel, stood. That long signature braid hung down one shoulder and she held her worn brown cowboy hat in her hands.

"What are you doing here?"

Rachel bit her lip. "I heard what happened."

This was a small town, and as the youngest of four girls, the baby of the family, Erin was used to her family stepping in to help her.

Rachel made her way in and glanced toward Willow, then back to Erin. "Thought you might need some help."

Erin bit the inside of her cheek to try to keep her emotions in check.

"How did you hear?" Erin asked, reaching for the last frame on her desk... Ironically the photo was a smiling Erin on her very first day of teaching. That twenty-two-year-old had a whole world of hopes and dreams laid out before her.

"Rosewood Valley isn't big. Doesn't take long for word to travel, especially when it comes to layoffs." Rachel stopped just on the other side of Erin's desk. "And I saw you pulling out of the alley from the feedstore and noticed missing boxes. I decided to come here when I put those pieces together."

Erin moved the half-full box from her chair and set it in the floor. Unable to keep up her strength anymore, she sank into the chair and tried not to admit defeat, but she was pretty close.

"I don't know what I'm going to do," Erin admitted on a whisper.

Rachel dropped her hat on the desk and came around, easing a hip on the edge of it. She took the photo and leaned down with determination in her bold green eyes.

"You're going to remember the girl in this picture," Rachel stated. "You're going to fight for her because you don't want to let her down."

Rachel's bold words hit hard, clutching at Erin's heart.

"I just don't know what to do," Erin repeated, shaking her head.

"You know all of us will help you," Rachel offered. "Now that the farm is doing well and the farm-to-table events are bringing in an actual revenue—"

"That's not what I mean." Erin shook her head and gestured toward Willow who still took her chore seriously. Erin lowered her voice. "I don't know how the foster process will work now that I can't prove employment. She's been through so much and I've only had her two days. The thought of her being bounced around again or sent back to those horrid conditions…"

Erin couldn't even think of that right now. She would do absolutely anything to prevent that from happening, no matter where she had to find employment. She wasn't too proud to work fast food or the local grocery store. Her family wouldn't let her lose Willow, though. They'd find her work on the farm, something for her to do to legally prove Erin had employment.

She swiped at the tear that had slid down her cheek. She hadn't allowed herself to cry just yet. She hadn't wanted to fall apart in front of Willow or have the little girl worry about anything else in her life. No child should fret about adult problems.

"I know you don't want to overwhelm Willow," Rachel murmured. "But I think now is a good time for a family dinner at the farm."

Erin had sent pictures of Willow to her family but had asked they not bombard her just yet. Erin wanted Willow to get used to the new place before introducing her into the massive family of four sisters, three brothers-in-law, a niece, Erin's parents, and a few rescued animals. All of that could be overwhelming for an adult, let alone a foster child with social anxiety.

Rachel glanced over her shoulder. "She's absolutely adorable, by the way."

Erin smiled and nodded. "She really is and so sweet."

"You're perfect for her." Rach turned back to Erin and set the photo on the desk. "So how can I help?"

Just that simple question sent a new wave of emotions through her and a fresh dose of tears filled her eyes. "I don't even know," Erin replied honestly. "I'm sure you have your own work to do."

"Right at this moment, helping you find your footing is my work."

Another tap on the door frame pulled Erin's and Rachel's attention to the opening. There stood Jenn and Violet, her other two sisters.

Erin immediately looked to Rachel. Rach simply shrugged.

"What? I had to text them," her oldest sister defended. "I figured this was an all-hands-on-deck type of situation."

Erin glanced toward Willow who now also stared at the doorway. Patting her cheeks dry, Erin came to her feet and pasted a smile on her face as she crossed the room.

"Willow, these are my sisters I told you about. Do you remember the pictures I showed you last night?"

Willow looked to Erin and nodded.

"They just came to see if they could help," Erin explained. "Do you mind if they help me? Or if you want this to just be a project for you and me, they can come another time."

Willow looked to the Spencer sisters, then back to Erin. She truly had no idea how this would play out, but there were times she had to let Willow have the lead and keep some control over her life. Erin hoped that would make the little girl feel safe in her new environment.

"Stay." The softest word slid through Willow's lips and Erin smiled.

"Okay, then. They will stay," Erin replied. "I bet they'd love to meet you if that's alright. But I'll have them stay over here with me and if you decide you want to meet them, you can come over. If not, that's just fine. Okay?"

Willow nodded and shifted her curious gaze to the three sisters staring in their direction.

As much as she didn't want to get into this with anyone, she appreciated her sisters being here for her. She should've known Rachel would text them. It was a wonder her parents hadn't showed up as well.

"Where can we start?" Jenn, second in the line of sisters, asked as she glanced around the room.

"I guess we need to know what stays and what goes," Violet, who was only a couple years older than Erin, chimed in.

Erin tucked her hair behind her ears and tried to focus on the job and not the emotional turmoil rolling inside her. "All the decorations are mine and any books other than a textbook would also be mine. We don't have to get it all cleared out today. I can make a few trips."

"Let's do it all so you don't have to worry about coming back?" Violet suggested. "Then maybe we can talk about what you'll do next."

Vi ran a small vet clinic and no-kill animal shelter. There wasn't a doubt in Erin's mind her sister would find work for her if possible. And Jenn ran a salon in town. Erin certainly didn't know a thing about cutting or coloring anyone's hair. But she'd sweep floors if she had to.

Erin gestured for her sisters to follow her to the other side of the room by her desk. Lowering her voice, she said, "I actually have something temporary and very low paying. I don't even know the pay, to be honest," she murmured.

"You lost your job and gained one all in the same day?" Jenn asked, crossing her arms.

She nodded. "Joe wants me to tutor his daughter."

The silence that filled the room could best be described as awkward, but their faces all held a look of shock and confusion.

"You don't mean Joe, as in... *Joe*. Do you?" Rachel asked.

Once again, uncontrollable emotions overcame her and Erin drew in a deep breath as she raked her hands through her hair. Her sisters knew their history and how heartbroken Erin had been when he left. They also knew he'd be returning home for a summer visit. But none of them knew when. Each of her sisters seemed to lean in a bit more around the desk, clearly more than intent on hearing about this unexpected reunion than anything else.

"He's back," Erin confirmed.

"With a *daughter*?" Jenn asked.

"And you already met up with him?" Vi asked at the same time.

"Was this meeting before or after you were let go and did he bring his wife with him?" Rachel tacked on.

"Wait. I didn't think he wanted kids," Jenn added on a muttered breath.

Erin sank back into her seat and attempted to rein in her mess of internal thoughts. "It's been a really trying day. Can we discuss Joe later?"

The threesome eyed each other and Erin held her breath as she looked from one to the other.

"Sure," Violet agreed, then held up a finger. "But don't think we aren't coming back to this topic. We're only letting you off the hook because of the bad day."

Erin didn't care the reasoning; she was just glad she didn't have to dive down the rabbit hole of feelings for the only man she'd ever loved. She wasn't even sure what she'd say considering she had no clue how she felt...but she needed to figure out how to be around him, because she'd be seeing him again very soon. All summer, in fact.

Chapter Three

"Can you believe they just let her go?"

Joe had heard his Gram mutter her disbelief over and over since Joe had filled her in on the news. Quite honestly he'd been shocked she hadn't heard already, but she'd been alone at the church putting ferns in place for Sunday and then had driven home. Granted right after he told her, her cell started blowing up with texts from her friends about the layoffs at the school.

Joe hadn't been gossiping, not one bit. He had genuinely been worried for Erin and what would happen now, not just financially but in regards to her foster daughter.

Seeing Erin after all this time had sent a jolt of awareness he hadn't expected. He knew coming back to Rosewood Valley would stir up past memories and an Erin encounter couldn't be prevented, but the impact of seeing her had shaken him more than he cared to admit.

After the way they'd ended things and his tearful departure, maybe he'd held on to some residual guilt he thought he'd long moved past.

As his Gram continued to mutter and shake her head, he couldn't help but admire her love of others. Even though she and Erin had had a rocky relationship since his departure, Gram always put love above all else. The woman also didn't look like she'd aged a bit other than her pixie-cut silver hair. She barely had a wrinkle around those crisp blue eyes and her petite frame still made him feel so large in comparison.

"I have to think the school board didn't want to make this decision," Joe stated, for at least the fifth time in the past hour. "And I'm sure they weighed every option before deciding. It's unfortunate, but Erin is young and smart. No doubt she's a great teacher, and I'm sure God will open the right door for her when the time is right."

He stared across the backyard as Ada took the bubble wand and spun in a circle to see if she could wrap herself in the iridescence. He couldn't help but smile at her innocence and love of life. God had opened this door for him to be a father. Joe hadn't been ready and hadn't known what he was getting into when he'd transferred churches in Senegal and not only inherited a financially impoverished church but also taken in the daughter of a couple who had been tragically killed just after Ada's birth. Joe had met Carter and Ellen King through their mission work. They'd all three become fast friends and Joe had been so happy for them when they were expecting their first child. When they'd asked if he could be on their will in case of any disaster, he agreed...never thinking that request would come to fruition.

Since they'd tragically passed, Ada knew no other parent than Joe, but he'd always made sure to keep photos of her parents around and tell her stories of their mission work. While he hadn't been ready to become a father, he was honored and humbled to fulfill their wishes and raise Ada as his own.

But times like this, he wondered if he was doing a good job or if he was making the wrong decision. She'd struggled in school since starting and he didn't know if she had a learning disability or if she just needed to learn in a different manner. He'd thought he'd chosen the right teacher to help with the basics, but Ada simply wasn't grasping things. He'd eventually been told it wasn't the kindergarten or first grade curriculum, but rather Ada had a learning disability that set her back about two years. He knew she needed help and he had hope that Erin had come back into his life right at this moment for that very reason.

The trials he'd gone through over the past several years made him stronger and he knew the role of fatherhood was God opening a door Joe had tried to keep closed. He'd never questioned that. When he and Erin had dreamed of growing old together, he'd thought for sure they'd travel the world as missionaries, but while he'd been busy making his own dreams, she had been doing the same.

They'd realized after graduation that love wasn't the only thing that could carry them. They had to stay true to not only themselves, but also to what God called them to do as individuals.

Unfortunately each of their callings took them in separate directions.

Yet here they were, temporarily anyway, together again. This time each with a daughter and even more obstacles. Joe had no clue where he was supposed to go next. The call to leave seemed so clear years ago, but now he wasn't hearing God's voice like he used to. Joe couldn't help but wonder if it was time for something else and he'd been on autopilot for so long he'd missed the signs.

"I'm surprised Erin came by," his Gram went on. "I had no idea she had a little girl now. I bet Erin's heart is so full. She will be a wonderful mother. We've had our differences, but she's a good woman."

Yes, there was no doubt about that. Once he moved, he knew for a bit his Gram was upset and thought Erin didn't fight hard enough to keep him here, but that was just hurt feelings talking. Gram knew his work was important and she supported him. But the minor rift and his departure had put a small wedge between the two women he'd loved most.

He hadn't yet told his Gram that Erin would be Ada's tutor while they were in the States. Clearly his Gram had been affected by the breakup but still held a special place for Erin in her heart. Now wasn't the time to mention the temporary teaching position. Once he and Erin had all the details worked out, he'd let his Gram in on the arrangement.

Ada continued to dip the wand into bubble mixture and enjoy the simplicity of her childhood. He knew she'd fit right in here in his hometown. Thankfully she was a well-rounded child and could adapt easily. It was the academics that concerned him, but this break from everything to visit family would be good for both of them. This would be the first time meeting Ellen's mom and Joe knew just how much this milestone meeting would impact both ladies.

Before he could think any more on that or reply to his Gram, his cell vibrated in his pocket. He pulled the phone out and almost let the call go to voice mail but opted to go ahead and answer.

"Sorry, Gram. This will just be a minute," he told her.

"Take your time," Garnet called back. She sat down her glass of lemonade and came to her feet, crossing the yard to play with Ada.

Joe swiped to accept the call. "Good afternoon, Robert." Joe greeted his mentor and lead pastor of the church he was affiliated with.

"I hope this is a good time to talk," Robert replied.

"Sure is. What can I do for you?" Joe asked, as if he didn't know exactly what this conversation would be about.

"I know we discussed your own startup church in West Africa and you're considering it, but I just found out that not only has housing been thrown into the mix, but also a one-on-one teacher for Ada. I know education was a big concern for you, but the village you would be going to has a ministry with English-speaking teachers from Canada. Ada would have all her academic needs met."

She would with Erin as well.

How did he know this for certain? Honestly he didn't. But for reasons he couldn't explain, and didn't want to explore at this moment, that was the first thought that came to his mind. Erin would pour herself into Ada and make sure his girl had all she needed. He didn't have one single doubt about that.

But what happened when summer was over? If he decided to go back to Africa and start up this new church from scratch, Ada would need assistance. How could he turn down a dream job helping people and a one-on-one education for Ada? He certainly hadn't expected a home *and* a teacher thrown into the offer.

"That's great to hear," Joe replied. "Her education is very important to me. With launching an entirely new mission plus trying to keep her home life stable… I have been worried about more than schooling."

"I'm trying to work out all the kinks on this end so that way this can be the easiest yes you've ever said."

Robert had every intention of getting Joe back in Africa, but something was holding Joe back. He couldn't put his finger on it, but he'd had to step away for just a bit to clear his mind and try to reconnect with his relationship with God, and focus on Ada. There was no better time or place than summer in his hometown. Being here with Gram was good for both his daughter and him.

After his own parents passed when he was little, his Gram took him in. Perhaps that was why he held his relationship with Ada in such a special place in his heart. He knew what it was like to grow up without parents and he wanted to cover her with as much love as possible.

Which was why this upcoming decision was so difficult.

"I appreciate you letting me know," Joe told his longtime friend. "Ada has to be one of my top concerns."

"As a father myself, I completely understand. I also know you need to take some time, but I want to keep you informed of everything."

The scene before him had Joe so thankful he'd chosen to come stay with his Gram for the summer. Not only was this good for his and Ada's hearts, but his Gram hadn't stopped smiling since they arrived. She'd been a widow for over a decade and the woman loved having people in her home…especially around her kitchen table. When Ada and Joe showed up, he didn't recall seeing his Gram that excited in all the years he'd known her. Having her family here and a new granddaughter to dote on had truly boosted her to a whole new level of happiness. And when Ada's other grandmother arrived in a couple weeks, Joe had a feeling both Gram and Ada would have permanent smiles.

Joe said his goodbyes and disconnected the call but remained on the wicker patio chair. It didn't seem like that long ago his Gram had been playing with him in this very yard. At one time there had been an old swing set and she would push him for hours. The woman never tired of playing with children. Her smile never faltered. The love of Jesus always beamed through her and he was beyond blessed to have her in his life.

The cell on the patio table chimed and Joe glanced over. His Gram's phone lit up with a name he certainly recognized. Matthew Book, the minister at the church in town.

His Gram laughed as she blew a bubble and Ada popped it with her little fingertip.

"Would you answer that for me, Joe?" she called, not even glancing his way as if she didn't want to miss a moment of time with her granddaughter.

Joe picked up the cell and answered.

"Hello, Pastor Book," Joe greeted. "Gram is a little tied up right now, but I can relieve her of this game of bubbles if you need me to."

Matthew chuckled. "No, that won't be necessary. It's actually you I wanted to talk to. I just didn't have your number."

Joe eased back in his seat. "Oh, well we can fix that."

He rattled off his number and reached for his own glass of lemonade. There were certain things he loved about being back in the States and so many things he took for granted when he lived here—like his Gram's perfectly sweetened lemonade.

"What else can I do for you?" Joe asked, then took a sip of the cold drink.

Matthew blew out a long sigh. "Well, I'm in a bit of a bind and you were the first person I thought of. Now, let me preface this by saying I don't want you to feel obligated to say yes."

A twinge of concern niggled at him, but more curiosity than anything. "You've certainly got my attention." Joe laughed.

Gram turned her head slightly. No doubt her ears perked up. She might be a good Christian woman with high morals, but she also loved to know all the ins and outs of everything going on…with him and everyone else. She kept dipping the wand in and holding it out for Ada to blow bubbles, but that woman was definitely taking in every single word.

"I need you to keep this conversation strictly between us," Matthew started. "I plan on retiring later in the fall. This isn't a decision I take lightly and certainly one I've prayed over." Joe could understand praying hard over a decision. "My wife and I will continue to support the church and be used where we are needed, but I need to step down from the pulpit. I think it's time for someone younger to step in."

That bundle of nerves in Joe's belly tightened. He knew where this was going.

"I know there's no way you can give me a decision today," he went on. "And there are many details to discuss, but I wanted to plant the seed and give you time to think. Garnet told me you were home for the summer."

"I am," Joe confirmed, still stunned at this offer from out of nowhere.

Or was it? Nothing surprised God. Every step in life had been planned by Him. Joe just had to listen and figure out if he was taking the right steps. Was this offer the reason Joe had come back? Or was this offer just a means to weigh against his life in Africa? Africa was all Ada knew and he couldn't just uproot her without some serious prayer.

"I was hoping I could get you to guest preach a Sunday or two while you're home," Matthew stated. "Again, no pressure and no matter your decision to take over, I think the congregation would love to hear you."

That was an easy yes. Joe loved talking to people and sharing his ministry. Not to mention these were people who'd helped shape his life and supported him in so many ways.

"I'd be happy to take a couple of Sundays," Joe informed him. "Let me know the dates and I'll prepare my sermons."

"I'll do that. I'd like to sit down for coffee and lay out all the reasons you'd be the perfect fit for this position and what all the church would offer if you accept," Matthew went on. "It's difficult to make any decision without all the details to consider and of course the board would have to approve. But, with you being from here and the rural area, you are the perfect candidate."

Gram turned and met his gaze, then raised her brows as if she could tell what was going on. Knowing that woman, he figured she probably did. Very little happened around Rosewood Valley without passing through her ears or lips. She likely already knew Matthew wanted to retire and move on, but he had to let this idea settle in and he had to pray because now he had two solid options and he didn't take either of them lightly.

He had the summer to figure out what was best for him and Ada and he had to admit some of his decision hinged on how well she adjusted to life here in the States, the visit with her grandmother and progress with Erin.

She hadn't left his mind for the ten years he'd been gone and now that he was back, he had a feeling she'd be front and center once again. He wasn't sure how this would go or where his feelings would take him, but he wasn't eighteen anymore and he wasn't in a position to jump into any type of relationship. They were both older, more mature—not high school sweethearts with lofty dreams.

Reality had pulled them apart and Joe doubted anything would push them back together.

Erin kept the soft momentum going in the old rocking chair she'd been gifted from one of the elderly ladies at church. Willow had curled up on Erin's lap with the book from the classroom. This had been a stressful, trying, emotional day, but relaxing here in this moment with the sweetest girl eased some of Erin's worries.

Willow reached up and toyed with the charm on Erin's necklace and Erin brought the rocking to a halt. She glanced down to the small white pitcher charm between Willow's tiny fingertips.

"My mom got me this necklace," Erin explained. "All my sisters have one just like it. Did you see theirs today?"

Willow glanced up and nodded.

"My mom got these when we were all younger," Erin told her, setting the chair into motion once again. She closed the book and sat it on the side table, then rested her hand on Willow's pajama-clad leg. "The pitcher is to remind us we have to pour into ourselves before we can pour into others."

Willow's dark brows drew in and Erin smiled.

"Sounds confusing, but what that means is we have to make sure we are taking care of ourselves. That way we can care for other people. So I have to make sure I'm loving myself so I can love you. Does that make sense?"

Willow nodded and directed her attention back to the charm as she continued to roll it through her fingers. There was a fine line in regards to discussing family. Erin was thankful for the wonderful Christian family she'd been blessed with, but at the same time Willow hadn't been so fortunate. Erin didn't want to keep throwing that out there and reminding the young girl of what she didn't have. Little by little Erin hoped to integrate all the positives from her family and lifestyle into Willow's world so she could see the good and push all the bad and ugly to the back.

Willow's mother was gone and her father wasn't much good in her life now, and Erin still wasn't even quite sure of all the details. All Erin had been told was the father was in rehab and the mother had passed away. There were rumors of some drug issues and abuse within the home and Erin couldn't even imagine what Willow had seen.

None of that would happen on Erin's watch. There would be bedtime stories, baking cookies, time spent on the family farm with horseback riding, and plenty of hugs and affection. Erin had to think that having another young girl around would also help. She'd need to take Willow with her during her tutoring sessions, and Ada seemed very outgoing and bubbly. That personality in a safe, controlled setting would be good for Willow.

But would being around Joe so much be good for Erin? She wasn't so confident in that, seeing as how her heart had beat just a tad faster the entire time she'd been with him earlier. She knew his stay here was temporary just as she knew his priority would be his daughter. Erin's priority had to be Willow.

And now finding a permanent job.

"Read?"

Willow's little one-word question cut through the thought that threatened to send Erin back into a panic. God never caused panic or worry so she knew those intrusive thoughts only stemmed from evil. She had to take her mother's advice and pour into herself before she could pour into Willow or anyone else.

"Let's finish this story and get to bed." Erin grabbed the book and turned to the page they'd left off on. "I have an extra special surprise for you tomorrow so you're going to want to get a good night's sleep."

Willow's eyes widened and she gave a small smile, as if she was afraid to get her hopes up. That was fine. Erin wouldn't get disappointed or upset. She would take baby steps and move forward each day to show Willow just how good the world could be and just how much love she deserved.

Erin finished the book and got Willow all settled into the cozy twin bed with fresh new bedding. Erin had bought the first set she'd seen and it just so happened to be pale blue with unicorns. The tiny spare room in Erin's house had been used for storing Christmas totes and her tree and a few seasonal things from her classroom, but all of that had gone into the shed out back. Thankfully her family had pitched in quickly and they had been amazing these past few days, giving necessary space so Willow and Erin could get acclimated with each other and Willow could adjust. The size of the Spencer clan alone could be intimidating, but Erin couldn't wait for the rest of the crew to shower Willow with the love and care she so desperately deserved and needed. No child should ever lack for hugs or affection.

She smiled at the girl. "Good night, Willow."

As Erin gently closed the door, leaving a slight crack, she let out a sigh. Today had been long, with one emotional jolt after another. She needed a nice hot cup of tea, her Bible, and some quiet time to pray and reflect. Tomorrow she'd have to call children's services and inform them of her drastic financial change. She didn't know what this would look like for the future, but she would beg, borrow, and do everything in her power to keep that child right here. God hadn't put them together just to rip them apart after only a couple of days.

Erin would put her worries behind her because having them front and center in her mind would get her nowhere. She would have faith, just like she'd had all along.

Chapter Four

"I remember getting baptized right over there."

Joe pointed to the trickling creek that ran behind the old white church where he'd grown up. Ada stood one side of him and Pastor Matthew stood on the other. Matthew had texted this morning to see if Joe would be interested in coming to the church to see the changes that had been made over the past ten years.

"I believe I was about your age," he went on as he glanced at Ada. "Best decision of my life, right next to adopting you."

Her wide smile spread across her face as she peered up at him. "It's like the river in Senegal."

Joe chuckled. "It is."

Their baptisms weren't that different here in Rosewood Valley compared to West Africa. They'd go down to the river if the person wanted to be submerged, or sprinkling was quite popular as well. Joe had done so many over the years and each one was special. An immediate image of him baptizing people right here, where his own life had changed so many years ago, popped into his head. Coming full circle—baptizing others in the place he'd been baptized—would be an amazing milestone, but he still wasn't sure this was the right move for him.

The friendships and deeply rooted bonds he'd made during his mission work were all life-changing. The dinners and small Bible study groups he'd hosted were so special although at times risky, considering the areas he'd been in. Not everyone could freely profess Christianity where he'd been, but spreading the Word had been his life and he'd made such progress, he felt guilty for even considering walking away from where God had led him.

"I'm sure things have changed a good bit since you were here last," Matthew added. "We've done some upgrades to the church itself, plus added this covered picnic area a few years ago. But I'm sure you're also wondering about housing and pay."

Joe nodded. "I'd like to say that's not important, but it is. I have to look at the full picture."

Ada tapped his arm and pointed toward the creek. "Can I go swing over there?"

The large tire swing swaying from a thick branch had captured her attention. "Sure," Joe said, "but don't get any closer to the water, please."

He kept his eye on her as she scurried off without a care in the world. Having Ada in his life had opened his eyes to so many things he never thought possible. Fatherhood, for starters. But her love for all the things and her loyalty coupled with that constant smile on her face only showed Joe that he needed to enjoy the simple things. While he worried about her education, he also realized that while she might not put studying as a top priority, she did place other people's feelings highest on that list... How could he be upset with that?

"She seems to love it here," Matthew stated once they were alone.

Ada climbed onto the swing and pushed off the fat trunk

to get going. She closed her eyes, tipped her head back, and held on to the rope as she swung back and forth.

"She's pretty adaptable, but she can also keep her feelings hidden." Joe turned his attention back to Matthew. "My decision will ultimately come down to what's best for her future."

"As a father of four, I get that," Matthew replied. "The parsonage that comes with the position is next door. The same house we've always owned."

Joe knew the cute little white cottage with a wraparound porch. The place had been a staple in town just like the white church that sat at the base of the hill. He'd been in a few times as a child when his Gram would go visit the then pastor's wife. The home had two bedrooms and two bathrooms, a living room and a kitchen. Nothing fancy, but enough for his and Ada's needs.

"The pay can be a little negotiable," Matthew continued. "Since I will be retiring soon and I haven't found a candidate that I think would be a good fit, we could discuss salary."

He threw out a number that was a little lower than what Joe felt comfortable with, but if he wasn't paying for a home, then perhaps everything would balance out. Again, something else to consider. And it wasn't like he lived a frivolous lifestyle. The biggest expense he had was Ada and the fact she wouldn't stop growing. He'd learned pretty quick that kids needed new clothes and shoes each season. One day things fit, the next their shoes were two sizes too small.

"I'm not sure if you ever thought of returning home permanently." Matthew shifted his stance and pulled in a deep breath. "I understand you came back to visit with Garnet and this opportunity came out of nowhere, but I have to believe God opened this door for you right at the time He opened another for me."

Was that what was happening? Or was God giving Joe options so he'd lean on Him more and dig deeper down for faith? He'd never thought of being a full-time minister in his hometown. The offer and idea definitely caught him off guard, but he'd worked so hard and for so long toward having his own mission organization in West Africa. He couldn't just ignore the need there.

Matthew gestured toward Ada who continued to drift back and forth on the tire. "She seems to be adjusting well."

"She's enjoying our vacation, which we haven't done before," Joe explained. "She loves all the greenery and the different homes. She's a social butterfly and thankfully I taught her English from the start so she's bilingual. French is more prominent in our town."

"She's an amazing little girl. You two seem like the perfect pair."

Joe couldn't help but smile. "We're just two imperfect people God put together, but I barely remember a time without her in my life. She's the missing piece I didn't know I needed."

"Kids will do that to you," Matthew replied with a chuckle. "I was always hesitant about having children, but once we had the first one, I realized I had been granted the greatest gift and then we had three more. There's never been a day in my life I've regretted marrying and starting a family. And there's no better place than Rosewood Valley."

A nostalgic tug pulled Joe's heart. His mind drifted back to the young man who'd stood at the crossroads of creating a family here with Erin or following his calling thousands of miles away. Where would he be had he stayed? Where would *they* be? Most likely they'd have their own children and he'd be a pastor. They'd do Sunday dinners at Four Sisters Ranch with her family and maybe Gram.

But he wouldn't have Ada and he didn't believe the move he'd made years ago was a mistake.

"I'm not trying to give you a sales pitch," Matthew went on. "I just couldn't imagine a better place to raise children. Granted no town, church, or community is perfect, but I'd like to think we're pretty close."

"Can we get one of these back home?" Ada called as she hopped off the swing and raced toward him.

Home. She thought of Senegal as home, while he still considered Rosewood Valley his.

"I'm sure we can find a spot for a tire swing," he assured her.

Her beaming smile warmed his heart and he knew he'd do anything to keep her spirit happy and thriving.

"I should probably get going," Joe stated. "You've given me a good bit to think about and no matter what happens, I'm honored you asked and I'm excited to preach in the church that helped shape me."

Matthew nodded. "I think filling in for me a couple of times will also help you make your decision. No matter what you decide, you have to do what's best for you and everything needs to be in God's plan."

Joe shook the man's hand and thanked him before escorting Ada across the paved parking lot behind the church and toward his rental car. She reached up to take his hand, as she often did, and he couldn't help but wonder when she'd feel too old to do such a thing. For now he'd cherish each special moment no matter how small. They were a team and all these heavy decisions weighing heavy on him had him worried. He didn't want to turn down the wrong path.

"I know you're probably nervous, but I'll be right here with you and I promise you're going to love the farm."

Erin had tried to reassure Willow all morning and again during the short car ride from their cottage to Four Sisters. Nerves curled within Erin. This would be the first time Willow truly saw part of Erin's world and met her parents.

"We have chickens and horses," Erin went on as she turned onto her family farm and drove beneath the white metal arch that read FOUR SISTERS. "And my mom always has something yummy in the kitchen. Sometimes it's pie, or cookies, or fresh bread. The bread is the best because my mother keeps homemade strawberry preserves on hand."

"I love strawberries."

The little voice from the back seat was so low Erin barely heard, but it was something. They were very slowly making progress in getting Willow to open up. A few sentences per day was a great improvement in the few days they'd been together.

"Me, too." Erin grinned. "Here we are."

She pulled toward the back door entrance where the family always went in and glanced in the rearview mirror. "Are you ready to meet my mom and dad?"

Willow's eyes widened and she squeezed her stuffed unicorn a little tighter to her chest.

Erin's heart squeezed at the worried gesture. She turned around in the seat to face Willow fully. "If you are uncomfortable or feel too nervous at any time, just reach up and squeeze my hand two times and that can be our little signal. Okay?"

Willow stared back without a word and Erin extended her arm to reach back. "Here. Let's practice."

Willow looked down at her outstretched hand for a moment before sliding her delicate little hand on Erin's.

"Now squeeze twice," Erin prompted.

Willow gave a couple of gentle squeezes and Erin nodded with encouragement.

"Just like that." Erin smiled with assurance. "Are you ready to go now that we have our secret code?"

Willow nodded and Erin stepped from the car and went to open the back door. Willow hopped down from her booster seat and continued to clutch her favorite toy. Erin took Willow's free hand and carefully led her toward the back door. Her own heart beat fast because she just didn't know how this interaction would affect Willow. Erin had to believe nothing but positive would come from today. Her parents were Godly people full of love and faith. God, love and faith were key components that could shape any child and Willow desperately needed all three. Erin could think of no better place than Four Sisters.

She moved up the few steps to the back door. As Erin clutched the knob beneath her palm, she glanced over her shoulder.

"We good?" she asked.

Willow nodded.

"Two squeezes if you need to go," Erin reminded her. "But I bet you're going to love my parents and the special surprise I have planned in a bit."

Erin didn't know of anyone, especially a child, who didn't love horses and a beautiful farm. Erin found that kids often felt more comfortable around animals as opposed to people because animals had no judgment and only affection. Another component Willow needed, but maybe she didn't even know it.

The moment Erin opened the back door, a waft of something yeasty yet sweet enveloped her. No scented candles or bowls of potpourri were needed in Sarah Spencer's kitchen.

The woman loved to bake and cook, and could can produce and throw together delicious goody baskets.

"There you are." Sarah wiped her hands on the bottom of the yellow apron that Erin had made for her years ago. "I just pulled some fresh sourdough bread from the oven and I made a new peach preserve last night. I'm changing up my recipe just a bit."

"That sounds delicious," Erin replied, then she turned to Willow. "Do you like peaches?"

Willow's eyes were locked on Sarah, but she nodded.

"Would you like to sit at the table or over here at the island and have your snack?" Erin asked. "My sisters and I always sit at the island because we want to see what all Mom is working on."

Willow said nothing but pointed toward the barstool on the end. Erin caught her mother's smile as Sarah stared down at Willow. Erin had already told her parents everything she knew about Willow and how timid and afraid the little girl was. All of this get-to-know-you phase would have to go slowly and they'd all have to let Willow be in control.

"I'm so glad you both came to visit." Sarah rested her hands on the old butcher-block island and continued to offer that sweet smile toward Willow. "My name is Sarah and I'm Erin's mom. And you're Willow?"

Willow looked down to her unicorn and poked the tip of the horn with her finger. She nodded, but kept her gaze averted from the stranger.

Sarah glanced toward Erin, then back. "Well, that is a beautiful name for a beautiful young lady. Does your unicorn have a name?"

Willow whispered something, but Erin couldn't quite hear her.

"Did you say Pickles?" Sarah asked.

Willow shook her head and Erin thought she noticed a little smile.

"Biggles?" Sarah asked. "Niggles?"

Willow let out a little chuckle but kept her head down and spoke just a bit louder. "Giggles."

"Oh, Giggles." Sarah made a show out of hearing correctly. "Well, that is a lovely name as well and I love all of her bright colors. So fun and festive. Now, would you like some bread and jam?"

Willow's big brown eyes darted up to Erin in a silent question.

Erin nodded. "I'm saying yes for sure. You can try it and nobody will be upset if you don't like it or want something else. Sound good?"

A long pause filled the cozy kitchen and Erin waited, wondering how Willow would respond. Ultimately, she nodded her head.

"Perfect," Sarah stated with a clap of her hands. "I'll have some, too. I've been so busy today I think I'll treat myself."

"Are you getting ready for the farmer's market or another event?" Erin asked as she took a seat next to Willow.

"Both." Sarah chuckled. "And your father asked for a special dinner so I was preparing for that as well."

"Is Dad in the barn?"

Sarah nodded. "Always something to do around here and he can't sit still too long, but he'll be up shortly. I made him promise."

Erin watched as her mother sliced the bread in even pieces and placed them each on a small plate. Willow seemed intent on watching and Erin had to believe all was well. So far, so good.

"Here you go." Sarah passed over two plates and kept

one for herself. "Now, I haven't tried this new recipe yet, so I want your honest opinions. You won't hurt my feelings if you don't like it."

"I'm sure it's delicious," Erin assured her. "Just like everything else you make. I can only remember one bad thing coming from this kitchen."

Sarah closed her eyes and shook her head. "Don't say it. I don't even want to think about it."

Erin laughed. "The meat loaf."

Her mother cringed. "It was horrid. I had to come up with something else quick when I had four little girls and a husband all waiting for dinner."

Erin laughed again as she picked up her bread. "I think that's when Dad took over kitchen duties. He thought you needed a break."

Her parents shared all chores both inside and outside the farm, but her mother loved cooking and baking so much everyone just let her be in her kitchen element.

"So, how's the bread and preserves?" Sarah asked.

Erin glanced to Willow, who had nearly eaten her entire piece already, then smiled at her mother.

"Well, I guess this new recipe is a hit," her mother stated with a confirming nod. "Would you like another piece?"

Willow glanced at Erin.

"You can tell her yes if you want," Erin stated softly, hoping to encourage more communication. "My mom loves to feed people and there's plenty."

"Yes, please," Willow murmured.

Erin breathed a sigh of relief. Just as Sarah reached for the knife to slice another piece of bread, the back door opened and Erin shifted in her seat. Will Spencer, her father, stepped over the threshold and removed his worn brown cowboy hat and hung it on the appropriate peg just inside the door.

"You're just in time," Sarah stated. "A little afternoon snack."

"Can't wait," Will grunted.

Her father could sound a little gruff at times, but the man was the epitome of a big teddy bear. He'd raised four girls so there was no way he could do that and not have a huge soft heart.

"Willow, this is my dad."

Erin turned to the little girl only to find Willow's eyes wide and both hands clutching her unicorn.

"Willow?" Erin asked softly.

Without taking her eyes off Erin's father, Willow reached forward and took Erin's hand and squeezed two times.

Chapter Five

"And then we just add the letter *S* if we're talking about more than one dog."

Joe tried not to listen in on the tutoring session between Erin and Ada, but considering her home was so small, there really wasn't much else to do. He and Erin decided that meeting at her place might be better for Willow so she could stay in a more familiar environment while Erin was busy.

Joe had brought his laptop so he could work on his sermon. Erin had given him a spot in the living room with a little corner desk while she and Ada sat at the kitchen table. The small two-story cottage seemed to fit Erin's personality. A mix of bright colors and mismatched furniture that all seemed to just work together. The open floor plan made it easy to see the duo working hard. Willow sat at the table as well, but she was coloring a few sheets that Erin had printed for her.

Joe stared at the blinking cursor and willed the right words to come. Preaching on coming home should be easy…yet he struggled. Discussing coming home to Rosewood Valley and tying in going to the final home with God had been his plan, but here he sat with nothing more than ideas and bits and pieces bouncing around inside his mind.

Nothing formed together that would hold anyone's attention. He couldn't even hold his own at this point.

He eased back in the seat and glanced around, still trying not to be intrusive on the tutoring session. As he scanned the room, he took in more details than the initial bright decor. Now he saw the love Erin had poured into her home. The variety of photos lining the mantel, the artwork secured with magnets on her fridge, and the random toys sitting around really showed just how much Erin not only loved her life, but that she was thriving at motherhood.

The invisible vice grip around his heart clenched...and not for the first time since he'd arrived. There were so many memories, so much nostalgia in this town, almost as if everything was waiting on him to return. Yet here he was making new memories with his daughter and the woman he'd left behind. He never thought the worlds would collide like this and he wasn't quite sure how he felt about the myriad emotions.

Looking at Erin at her little table with four chairs, and three of them full, only proved they had indeed moved on. Life had kept going here, just like his own had continued overseas.

And yet life had brought him back here, with his daughter in tow. Ada was getting the chance to see what his upbringing had been like, spending time with Gram and exploring Rosewood Valley. And next week, she'd meet her maternal grandmother for the first time.

"Are these right?" Ada asked.

Erin sighed and pursed her lips. He knew that look. She'd always done that when she didn't want to answer a question or if she had something negative in her mind. Erin would never do anything to purposely hurt someone's feelings and he had no doubt she wasn't about to start now.

"You did really well on these first two," Erin started as she pointed to the paper. "Then they started getting tricky, didn't they?"

Ada nodded. "I want to understand and be smart."

Erin covered Ada's little hand with her own. "Oh, honey, you are so very smart already, not to mention you're a world traveler. How many seven-year-olds can say that? You can speak two languages and you smile when you speak. That makes people feel happy and comforted. Not many adults have that quality. In my opinion, you have many more important things going for you than making nouns possessive."

Joe's heart swelled. He obviously knew Ada was special and so precious, especially toward others. The fact that Erin had only been around her a short time and could already pick up on that warmed him. Erin had that nurturing side that couldn't be taught; she was just instilled with love, but she also embodied the perfect patience and care that a teacher should.

When Erin's eyes lifted and her gaze stretched across the room to meet his, Joe's breath caught in his throat. The slightly tipped corners of her mouth and the light in her gaze rendered him speechless. She wasn't frustrated with the session; she genuinely loved this moment and her servant's heart was more prevalent now than ever.

The kids in his town would adore her.

Wait. What? She wasn't coming back with him. She'd made her stance clear ten years ago. Her home was, and forever would be, Rosewood Valley. He had to respect that decision both then and now. At least he had to assume her position remained the same, considering she still lived here. Her roots ran deep in this town and someone like Erin would want to stay close to her family.

"So you think I'll get this?" Ada asked, breaking the moment.

"Yes." The littlest voice from Willow stunned Joe. He jerked his attention to the quiet girl still coloring, and Erin laughed.

"See? Even Willow knows you're smart," Erin confirmed. "You just need to believe it yourself. I always tell my students, if you knew everything already, you wouldn't need school. There's so much in this world to learn, so don't get frustrated or you'll miss all the good stuff."

"Like nouns?" Ada asked, scrunching up her face.

Erin tapped her fingertip to the end of Ada's nose. "Nouns and so much more."

Joe turned back to his computer and tried to focus on his own work instead of getting mesmerized by his high school sweetheart. But that blinking cursor continued to mock him.

"Willow, can you help Ada for just a minute if she runs into trouble?" Erin asked. "I just need to talk to Joe."

Willow glanced up, her eyes wide.

"You can do it," Erin encouraged. "You both are very smart girls and putting both of your heads together will get these exercises done in no time."

Erin didn't wait for Willow to shake her head or worry anymore. She turned toward Joe, knowing that pushing Willow just a bit outside her comfort zone with a girl nearly her age would be good for her. And the girls bonding would only benefit both of them.

She made her way across the room where Joe continued to stare at the white screen. As she neared, she realized he had a title to something, but nothing else. Clearly he struggled internally as well. They were all dealing with something yet trying to hold it all together.

Erin let out a sigh as she leaned a hip on the edge of the desk. Joe's bright blue eyes came up to meet hers...and just like that the young teen head over heels in love resurfaced. She had a flash of another time, another place. Of riding back roads in his old beat-up truck when he'd take her hand and flash her a smile. Of dancing at their high school prom when he'd looked into her eyes and promised they'd be together forever.

"What did you need to discuss?" he asked.

Erin blinked and pulled herself from the past and back into the moment.

"Oh, I don't need anything," she whispered so the girls couldn't hear "I just want both of them to do something that makes them slightly uncomfortable. That's the only way children grow. Willow might talk a bit more with a child than an adult and Ada might relate more to Willow showing her some things. The work we're doing with Ada is two grades below her level just so I can get a foundation for what we're dealing with, so Willow would have done this before."

Joe continued to stare and the unsettling silence niggled at her nerves. She didn't know how he could still manage to mesmerize her with something as simple as a look, but he did.

"You're pretty incredible at dealing with children," he finally said. "Not just as a teacher but digging deeper to find what works for them as individuals."

Erin shrugged. She wasn't much for compliments on something that everyone should do. It wasn't difficult to listen to and gauge what works for a child. Kindness was a free trait everyone should tap into, especially when dealing with the next generation.

"It's my job," she replied automatically, then the harsh reality hit her. "Or it was, anyway."

"And it will be again," he assured her.

Joe shifted in the desk chair to face her fully. Erin eased off the edge and stood straight up, trying not to get too close. She couldn't get too comfortable with this man again. Their conversations and any dealings they had while he was in town had to remain superficial. Even though they were completely different people now and had lived ten years apart, Joe wasn't staying and there was no reason for her to be naive enough to think he was here for any other reason than to visit. At this point in her life, she didn't think she could handle another heartache if she got too close and had to watch him leave again.

"From your lips to God's ears."

She crossed her arms and glanced toward the girls. Ada continued to work, but Willow was watching carefully.

"Ada is a very bright little girl," she told Joe. "So many kids sometimes look as if they're falling behind, but they all work at different speeds. Usually around middle school they all start catching up to each other. So don't be so hard on yourself or worry too much. She might be a little behind, but comparing kids to other kids isn't fair to anyone. It's like saying a fish is dumb because it can't climb a tree. But they weren't made to climb trees, they were made to swim. Maybe Ada was made for more than spelling and grammar."

Joe tipped his head as his brows drew in. "I've never heard anyone phrase education like that before."

Erin crossed her arms and glanced back to the table. "That's because everyone tries to have a blanket statement that applies to all kids," she said as she turned her attention back to him. "But I assure you, not all kids are the same. It's difficult to find two that are alike, let alone an entire classroom."

"So you think she'll be okay?" he asked, the worry undeniably lacing his tone.

Erin couldn't prevent the instinct to reach out and console him. Her palm covered his on the desk before she could think twice. That familiar warmth from his large hand beneath hers took her back once again. How many times had she held that hand as a teen? How many times had he taken hers whether to comfort or just out of the need to have a connection?

And how many lives had he touched in the ten-year gap since he'd been gone? He'd lived a whole other life that had nothing to do with her, yet this touch that had been so familiar at one time made her realize that while they did share a bond, they were quite different people.

"Ada will be perfectly fine," she assured him with a gentle squeeze before she forced herself to pull away. "It's not unusual for children to need help every now and then. Besides, she has social skills that so many kids don't and that is something that can't be taught."

Joe's soft grin replaced the worry lines between his brows. "She's always been with me when I visit people in our village and she's a great little hostess when we have people into our home for Bible study or just dinner."

Joe nodded in the girls' direction. The two had their heads close together as they were chatting, followed by a little giggle.

"Willow seems to be adjusting well. It looks like she's speaking a bit more to Ada than I've seen."

Erin pulled in a deep breath as her own fears threatened

to consume her. "That's another reason I wanted her to help Ada right now. Willow doesn't speak much and earlier today she got scared at my parents' house when she saw my dad and we had to leave."

Joe jerked his attention back to her. "Your dad? Will Spencer is one of the kindest men I've ever known."

Indeed he was, but the way Willow had instantly needed to leave left Erin worried. Erin had told her parents she needed to get home and she'd call them later. She'd ended up texting them once she got Willow settled at home and said she'd try again another day.

"I'm not sure what triggered her," Erin whispered. "We made a secret code for when she's nervous or scared and needs out of a situation. She did that immediately when he walked in and spoke to her."

Joe shook his head. "I don't understand, but I'd guess somewhere along the way a man has been unkind to her and your dad might look like him or sound like him. Just a guess, though."

Erin assumed as much as well, which really worried her. "I left a message for her social worker and asked her to call me back," Erin said. "I know there are certain things I'm not allowed to be filled in on but I just need to know what I'm dealing with so I don't purposely put her in an uncomfortable position where she doesn't feel safe. I've been given most of her backstory, but there are still pieces I don't even think CPS is aware of."

"I never realized how fortunate I was with my adoption," he stated with a shake of his head. "I was on the will as Ada's guardian if anything happened to her parents and she was only a few weeks old when tragedy struck."

Erin jerked slightly and blinked at his statement. "I assumed Ada was biologically yours. I mean, I guess I just thought you and your...wife."

Joe tipped his head and offered a genuine smile that warmed her and made her giddy all at the same time.

"I've never married," he informed her. "And I wasn't lying when I left and said I wasn't ready for fatherhood. My mission work still came first and that's how I met Ada's parents. We were best friends, so I assumed the role of guardian on what I thought would be paper only. I never dreamed this would be how I became a father."

Erin's heart cracked and hurt for the man who wasn't ready to be a father, but stepped up when he was most vulnerable after losing his best friends. Dealing with grief plus a new life role had to have been so difficult.

And that testament right there proved what a remarkable, one of a-kind man Joe truly was.

"I had no idea," she murmured. "I'm sorry for your loss, but Ada is so blessed to have someone like you."

Joe nodded toward Willow. "And she's blessed to have you," he told her. "Maybe you're lucky to have each other since you're both going through a rough time. Ada actually helped me heal. Maybe you and Willow were put together to lean on each other."

"Maybe so," she agreed as her eyes drifted to her sweet girl.

"How's the job search coming?"

Erin smoothed her hair behind her ears and resisted the urge to groan as she directed her attention back to Joe. "Not well. That's another reason I need to speak to Willow's social worker. I left a message when I got laid off, but she was on vacation. My worry for Willow's placement trumps anything with my job."

"Something will happen soon," he assured her. "Keep

the faith until then and be sure to tell them you're tutoring until you get back to full-time."

Erin planned on just that, but tutoring wouldn't cover the bills once her savings ran out. Not to mention her car wasn't going to make it much longer. Her family had been on her to get something more reliable for months now, but she'd been trying to hold on to her funds for fostering.

Willow kept her going, though. Even when Erin felt like there was no way out of this situation or there seemed to be no answer, the little girl deserved someone who wouldn't give up and would fight the battle on her behalf. Erin fully intended to be that person no matter what.

"How was the tutoring?"

Gram breezed in the front door and hung her purse and keys on the hook before turning her attention to Ada. Joe glanced up from the book he was reading to see how she'd answer. Ada sat on the floor, using the coffee table as a desk to color one of the papers Erin had given her for fun.

"I don't feel as dumb as I did," Ada stated, putting her crayon down and coming to her feet. "Erin said I'm really smart."

"Well that's because you are," Gram enforced.

Ada crossed the room and threw her arms around Gram's waist for a big hug. That's just how his girl was. Always loving, always eager to be social and friendly. Erin was right. That was something that just couldn't be taught and much more important than a letter grade.

"Willow came, too," Ada stated as she stepped back. "She sat with me the whole time and I gave her one of my hair bows because she said how she liked the one I had. So since I had two, I thought we could be matching."

"That is very nice and so sweet that you already made a friend."

Joe closed his book and sat it on the table next to the chair and chuckled. "They get along really well. Ada chatters and Willow listens."

"Willow is super smart," Ada added with wide eyes. "She's a whole year younger than me and she already knows so much stuff."

Joe came up and rested his hand on Ada's shoulder. "That's why you two are so perfect. There are things you are good at that you can teach her, and she can teach you what she's good at."

"Does she have time to teach me everything before we go back home?" Ada asked in all seriousness.

This wasn't the first time Ada had brought up going back home. No doubt she was anxious to get back to her friends and her familiar surroundings.

"I'm not sure Willow can teach you everything, but I'm sure Erin will do all she can to make sure you feel more confident and ready to dive back into your education."

"I like Erin," Ada added. "She's really pretty and she smells good."

Yeah. She was all of that. Joe hadn't been able to dodge that familiar floral scent of hers. Even ten years later she still loved that floral scent and there was no denying her beauty. She had a natural grace and attraction that was impossible to ignore.

"She's always been a very pretty lady," his Gram chimed in. "Erin and her sisters are all lovely women."

"How many sisters does she have?" Ada asked, looking to Gram.

"There's three, four girls in total," Gram replied. "That's why they have a farm called Four Sisters."

"A farm?" Ada bounced up on her toes. "Like with horses and cows and chickens?"

Gram laughed. "They have all of that."

"Can we go see them?" Ada clapped her hands and looked from Joe to Gram and back again. "Can we?"

Joe wasn't sure how to answer that. Will and Sarah Spencer would open their home to anyone at any time, he was sure. But did he just invite himself and ask the parents of his ex if he could swing by? Did he go straight to Erin?

"Can we?" Ada repeated.

"I'll see what I can do," he assured her, then shifted his attention to Gram.

She simply smiled and nodded like this would all work out. He felt needy already having Erin help with tutoring, but he also was helping her out with a job so he shouldn't feel too bad. There were still all those unspoken words that seemed to hover between them, all the things they'd left unsaid so many years ago. Were they just going to ignore all of that and pretend that underlying hurt didn't still exist? Of course they'd moved on and created the lives they were obviously meant to have, but still...

Time seemed to linger around them, almost enveloping them closer together.

Like when her hand had slid over his earlier.

"You okay?" Ada asked.

Joe blinked and pulled himself from the memory. "I'm good," he assured his daughter. "What do you say we figure out what we can make for dinner and give Gram the night off?"

With Ada's grandmother arriving soon, Gram had been busy making preparations. Dottie would be staying several weeks, and Gram had gone above and beyond to prepare meals in advance and get the guest room ready. He loved his grandmother for that, but he wanted her to slow down and take a break.

"Oh, you don't have to do that," his grandmother insisted with a wave of her hand. "You know I love to cook."

"I'm aware, but you've been running errands all day and Ada and I know our way around the kitchen pretty well. Don't we?"

The girl nodded and took Gram's hand to lead her to the recliner Joe had just vacated.

"Here," Ada insisted. "You sit here and watch your favorite show or take a nap or read. We'll let you know when everything is ready."

Gram laughed as she took a seat. "Well, I've never been ordered by a seven year old, but I do like your determination."

Ada turned to Joe. "Let's go."

She marched toward the kitchen like she owned the place and Joe simply shook his head.

"She's impossible not to adore," his Gram said. "And you know you're going to have to take her to the farm."

Joe sighed. "Yeah. I know. Just trying to figure out the best path to take for that."

Gram tilted her head and offered the sweetest smile, her signature one that crinkled the corners of her bright blue eyes. "Honey, that family holds no grudges and they understand the reason you left. Everyone has moved on, including you."

True, so why did he still feel so stuck in the past from the moment he saw Erin again?

Chapter Six

"Can you put those pink flowers in the hole you just dug?" Erin pointed toward the planter on the back patio. "You did such a good job with the ones on the front porch."

Erin sat the flat of flowers she and Willow had grabbed from the feedstore earlier. She'd even bought a small pair of gardening gloves for the girl to wear. Willow had chosen a purple pair with little clusters of grapes on them. She looked too cute with her dark curly hair back in a ponytail and the bow Ada had so sweetly given her earlier today just before they'd left the tutoring session.

"I thought I heard you back here."

Erin turned and shielded the late afternoon sun from her eyes as Beth Graham stepped through the back gate. The social worker popping in unannounced was something Erin knew would happen during the fostering process.

"We were just planting some flowers," Erin explained. "Come on back."

Erin's nerves started curling in her belly. Not because of the visit itself—Erin knew she was doing a good job as far as love, support, and safety for Willow went—it was more the financial talk she'd have to have that made her so uncomfortable.

"These are beautiful," Beth commented as she stepped toward the concrete patio. "Hello, Willow."

"You remember Miss Graham, right, Willow?" Erin asked.

Beth was always so gentle with Willow and soft-spoken. Her petite frame and kind brown eyes made her a perfect person to deal with traumatized children.

Willow nodded and picked up a container of pink impatiens. Erin watched as she carefully removed the plastic and placed the roots into the little hole she'd dug in the potting soil.

"She seems to be adjusting well," Beth stated. "Everything going okay? I got your call, but knew I needed a visit so thought we'd just knock it all out at once."

There was no way to skirt around this topic or lie about it. She would face this battle head-on and find a solution in Willow's best interest.

"I'd rather discuss my issue in private," Erin murmured. "If you want to do that now or if you need to talk to Willow first, I'm fine either way."

Beth's brows drew in. "You seem concerned. Is she doing okay?"

Erin couldn't help but smile. "She's doing great. I started tutoring and she came along with me and she even helped some. She's found a nice bond with Ada."

"Oh, Ada," Beth interrupted. "Joe's little girl?"

Erin nodded, not a bit surprised at Beth's knowledge. This town was so small that news didn't stay isolated for long.

"Yes," Erin confirmed. "She and Willow have become little buddies."

She turned to face Willow. "Hey, sweetie. Show Miss Graham your new bow from Ada."

Willow patted down the dirt around her flower and came to her feet. She removed her little grape gloves and pointed toward her ponytail.

Beth gasped with delight. "Well, that is beautiful. How lovely to get a little present."

Willow smiled. "I like her."

"That's so important to have friends we like and can have fun with," Beth said. "And you're a great friend for helping her with her work."

Willow nodded, obviously proud of herself. Erin's heart swelled. The very little speaking Willow had done since she came was concerning, but more and more she saw a light starting to shine brighter in her big brown eyes. Any type of progress was a step in the right direction and Willow had only been here a few days. When she'd first arrived, all she wanted to do was hug her unicorn and refused to make eye contact with anyone. Erin felt fortunate that Willow felt safe enough to sit on her lap to read stories and sing bedtime songs. Establishing a routine had likely helped with the tough transition from the only home Willow had ever known.

"I'm going to talk to you when you get done planting your pretty flowers if that's okay," Beth told Willow. "I need to talk to Erin for just a minute."

Willow nodded and promptly put her little gloves back on, then went back to work.

"She's dedicated." Beth laughed.

"I have found she likes to be helpful." Erin led the way across the yard toward a shaded area in the back corner with a small table and chairs. "I assume she wants to feel needed so I try to give her things that are still fun, but that are sometimes a chore. I have found she loves folding towels."

"That's a great thing," Beth commended as she took a

seat. "And you're right. She wants to feel needed and like she's doing something good. From what I can understand, she hasn't been praised or shown positive examples. I was also given information just this morning from a family member that Willow was also always told to shut up. Supposedly she would be sent to her room with her food, her homework, or for anything. She wasn't typically allowed out with her parents."

Erin's heart hurt for the little girl. She couldn't imagine always being in a bedroom with nobody to talk to or other kids to play with outside of family get-togethers. Erin knew she'd grown up blessed. She'd seen enough children come through her classroom who weren't as fortunate. That was the whole reason she'd wanted to foster...well and because she'd always wanted a family, but she didn't even date much so the prospects of marrying and having kids wasn't in her near future.

"Is that why she doesn't speak much?" Erin asked.

"One would have to assume." Beth nodded. "She'll get there, though. I can't think of anyone better to help her through this dark time. I'm sure she misses her parents, though. As ironic as that sounds, children usually pull away more when they are removed from the only life they've ever known. After her mother passed, all she had was her father and now that's been removed. You and I know it's better for them somewhere else, but there's a fine line in getting children to understand that and embrace the positives when they've only known heartache."

Erin directed her attention to Willow who had the last pink flower in hand, trying to decide the best placement in the pot. There was no more stalling. She had to bring up the topic she and Beth needed to discuss.

"I was laid off from my job at the school," Erin blurted

out. "There were some budget cuts and I knew the school had a financial burden, but I had no clue there would be employees cut."

Beth eased back in her seat and sighed. "That's what the urgent call was about."

Erin nodded, even though Beth hadn't asked, she'd simply connected the dots and made a statement.

"I should have notified you the moment I found out, but I was thrown for such a loop and then I had to empty my classroom and Joe offered me a job and—"

"Joe gave you a job?" Beth asked. "Isn't he here only a short time?"

Erin nodded. "He is, but Ada needs tutoring. I've got some résumés out to other schools and I will find something, plus I have savings, and at the farm I help with farm-to-table events. I just don't want Willow to suffer for this and I don't want her removed."

"Relax." Beth smiled, reaching across the small table, and patted Erin's hand. "This is going to be a day-by-day situation. I'm not in the business of ripping children away from caring, loving homes. I know she's in the best hands with you and there's not a doubt in my mind that you'll find something. If Willow is still with you in another month and you haven't found work, we'll revisit this and see where we stand. But I will need you to keep me updated often, even if there's nothing to report, just so I can keep notes on the situation."

A flood of emotions washed over Erin. The first being worry. She didn't want to think of a time when Willow was taken away. And a month? That wasn't enough time to pour all the love into this child that she needed. But Erin had gone into the foster care with her eyes wide open, knowing full well she could, and likely would, get her heart broken.

If a child had the promise of a better life and a hopeful future in another home, then any pain Erin endured would be worth the trials.

On the other hand, a wave of relief slid through her, knowing her lack of permanent employment wouldn't have Willow removed immediately. The clock was ticking, though, and Erin needed to keep forging ahead on that job hunt. But in a small town, there weren't many options and she would have to expand her search.

"I'm going to talk to Willow for a bit alone and then I'll bring you in," Beth told her as she came to her feet. "But don't worry. We both want what's best for her and I wouldn't blindside you with anything."

Erin had a sense of reassurance. She'd overcome one obstacle but had many more to face. Prayer and her family would get her through this, she had no doubt. Erin's main concern was making sure Willow came through on the other side with the best life possible. While Erin hoped that would be with her, she had to be open to the possibility it might not be.

"This is just so exciting," Gram stated as she stared out the large picture window.

Joe couldn't believe the day had finally come for Ada's other grandmother to meet them. He'd hired a private driver to bring her from the airport to Gram's house so they could all meet her at the same time. Ada had insisted on wearing the pretty pink dress her biological grandmother had purchased and sent for her last birthday. And with her hair up in a curly pony and matching pink bow, she was simply too cute. Joe knew she was both a bundle of nerves and excited. He felt the same. He'd never met Ellen King's mother, so this would be a little bittersweet.

A black car pulled slowly into the drive and Ada let out a squeal and ran to fling open the front door. Joe smiled at Gram as they both made their way out to the front porch.

"You're here!" Ada's shout of delight had Joe and Gram laughing.

Dottie Banks had barely stepped her foot from the car when Ada ran to her. They'd had so many video chats over the years that Dottie certainly didn't feel like a stranger.

Ada threw her arms around her other grandmother and Dottie returned the loving gesture.

"Her world is complete now," Gram whispered. "How precious is she, putting that much love into her family?"

Emotions balled up in Joe's throat at seeing his daughter's happiness, and all he could do was nod.

"She's a blessed girl to have this many people who love her," Gram went on. "And I'm blessed you are sharing her with me."

Dottie and Ada started over toward them as the driver got the suitcases from the trunk and placed them on the driveway.

"Well, we finally meet in person," Dottie stated with a sigh as she held Ada's little hand.

The elderly woman was taller than Joe had thought from pictures and video chats. Her thin frame, long silver hair, and brightly colored clothing reminded him of that free spirit vibe, much like what Ada had.

"We're so glad you could make the trip." Joe stepped forward and offered a hug before easing back with a smile. "Come on in and I'll bring in your bags."

"And I'll show you your room," Ada offered.

Joe stepped aside as Gram moved into the mix.

"It's so lovely to meet you," Gram stated. "I'm Garnet."

Dottie pulled Garnet into a sweet embrace. "It seems we have a special little girl to spoil."

Gram laughed as she stepped back and glanced at Ada. "That's our job now."

Joe thanked and tipped the driver, then grabbed Dottie's bags as the man got back into his car. For a moment Joe stood and watched as the trio of ladies headed into the house. Not for the first time, he thanked God for this circle that enveloped Ada. She might not remember her parents, but that didn't make her void any less real. He wanted her to have all the love and support and guidance. There was no doubt with his own truth and loyalty to God and with the strong Godly women in her life, Ada would grow up rich in her faith and have that firm foundation. There was nothing else he wanted more than that.

Except perhaps a wife and mother to complete their circle.

"Good morning."

Erin greeted the elderly couple as she held the door open for them to enter the church on Sunday morning. She had asked Pastor Matthew if she could be one of the greeters so she could help Willow acclimate to socializing with positive people. The couple greeted in return before passing to take a seat in the church.

Willow stood right next to her as other churchgoers entered. The little girl would occasionally smile at the people milling in through the old wooden double doors.

"You know, I used to stand next to my mom and help like this when I was your age," Erin told Willow. "I always liked to shake hands. Would you like to shake anyone's hand as they go by? You don't have to say a word. I'll greet and you shake. Does that sound fun?"

Willow stared back with those dark brown eyes and ultimately nodded, sending her dark curls bouncing around her shoulders.

The next family that came in, Erin greeted them with a grin and turned to watch as Willow graciously extended her little hand.

The crowd seemed to be thinning out and Erin thought everyone was in, but just as she started to step from the door, Joe came around the corner escorting Garnet. Ada came up behind him, holding hands with a woman Erin didn't recognize. But then she remembered the special visitor that was coming to town.

This must be Ada's maternal grandmother.

"Good morning." Erin greeted the crew with a smile as they came up the steps. "You all look great today."

She tried to shift her attention among the foursome, but her eyes kept drifting back to Joe, who wore a dark suit with a crisp white shirt. No cowboy hat today out of respect for being in church, but he'd parted his hair just like she remembered, and her mind played tricks on her, trying to push her back to the past.

"You look pretty," Ada chimed in as she reached the doorway. "I like your dress, Erin."

Erin did a mock curtsy. "Well, thank you. You look quite adorable today in your pink flowers."

"And Willow has pink, too," Ada added. "It's like we're sisters."

Erin glanced to Joe at that statement and found his eyes locked on her as well. Such innocence from his daughter, yet the words held so much weight. The weight of what-ifs. At eighteen she'd dreamed of having kids with Joe who would share the same sibling bond she had with her own sisters.

He held her stare with an intensity that certainly didn't help her nerves or her constant attempt to remind herself they had both moved on.

"I'm Dottie."

Erin blinked from her thoughts and pulled herself back to the present. The newcomer held out her hand to shake and had a wide grin across her face.

Erin shook hands with the woman and nodded. "It's so nice to meet you. I'm Erin and this is Willow."

She pulled her hand back and gestured to Willow who also extended her hand.

"Good morning," Dottie replied. "It's so nice to meet Ada's friend. She has talked about you nonstop since I got in yesterday."

Erin had no doubt. Ada loved to chat. She and Willow had been getting along in tutoring and the two were quite adorable. Erin didn't miss the look of surprise and delight that flashed across Willow's face at Dottie's mentioning that Ada hadn't stopped talking about her.

"We better get inside," Garnet stated. "We're already running late and I just know Mrs. Hazelmyer will have stolen my seat again."

"I doubt the Lord cares where you sit to sing songs and listen to the Word," Joe replied with a chuckle.

Garnet ignored him and shook Erin's and Willow's hands. "You ladies look lovely this morning, but I will have to chat after the service."

Garnet moved on in and Dottie shrugged. "I guess we have to find some seats."

"I'll sit by you and maybe Willow can sit by us, too," Ada stated as she took Dottie's hand once again.

Willow glanced at Erin and Erin nodded. "Go on in and sit with Ada. I'll find somewhere close in a bit."

Willow hesitated, but ultimately went on in with Dottie, Garnet and Ada.

"Gram thinks she has to sit in the same seat every single service," Joe murmured as he stayed behind.

"That's how most people are," she replied. "Nobody likes being taken out of their comfort zone, especially in church."

He shrugged good-naturedly. "It's hard to grow in life without getting out of those zones," he replied.

Erin shifted her attention from the four ladies walking to their seats and back to Joe who had his eyes focused right on her. Did he mean she wasn't stepping out enough? Because she'd been out of her comfort zone since Joe returned.

"Would you like to sit with me?" he asked.

Her stomach knotted with anticipation. What would people think if they sat together? Would there be assumptions they were a couple once again? Or would anyone even care?

"I'm not sure," she answered honestly.

Joe's lips quirked into a side grin, which did nothing to help her giddiness and nerves.

"We're friends, Erin. Friends can share a pew in church, right?"

Friends. She'd once hoped for more, but their lives had taken them to different places. Now she was focused on finding a job and taking care of Willow. Yet she worried about both of those things lately and supposed she could use a friend...

She pulled in a deep breath, trying to weigh her decision. She wanted nothing more than to say yes, but she didn't want to set the gossip mill going. At the same time, she couldn't live her life worried about what other people would or wouldn't say. On the bright side, her family wasn't here to ask her about it. There was a private event at Four Sisters this afternoon and the rest of the Spencer clan had attended the earlier service. Erin had already volunteered as greeter at this one.

She had to live each day to be pleasing to God and herself. That was all. Besides, she had nothing to feel guilty about sitting next to Joe. He would be leaving at the end of summer and she knew full well the outcome of this visit. They could be, and obviously were, friends.

Erin returned his grin and nodded. "We should try to sit close to the girls since I promised Willow."

He extended his elbow in a silent gesture to escort her. "I'm sure we can make that happen."

Erin slid her hand in the crook of his arm and pushed aside any worries. She didn't want any negativity interrupting her time in church or her time with Joe. This day would be full of positivity, nothing less, because she refused to let anything else steal her joy.

Chapter Seven

Joe held on to Ada's hand as they stepped into All Good Things several days later. The local feedstore had been a staple in Rosewood Valley for decades. Walt, the manager, was just another fixture in the town. Everyone knew him and if he didn't have something in stock, he'd order it.

Yet it wasn't Walt behind the counter but Rachel Spencer. Erin's oldest sister greeted them with a wide smile and he couldn't help but return the gesture.

"Well, I heard you were back in town but was starting to think it was just a tall tale," she joked as she stepped from behind the handmade cedar wood checkout counter. "It's about time you popped in."

"I heard you were part owner now," he stated as he crossed to greet her. "And married to Jack Hart. I forgot all about that guy when he'd come visit during the summers. How's he doing?"

Jack Hart's grandfather had owned All Good Things, but with his passing in the past year, Jack had come back to Rosewood Valley and taken over...and apparently found himself a Spencer sister. A feedstore owner and a cowgirl? Quite literally a match made in heaven.

Rachel closed the gap between them and wrapped her arms around him. He honestly hadn't known how the Spencer clan felt about him once he left, but he should've known they didn't hold grudges.

He used his free arm to give her a hug.

"And who is this?" Rachel asked as she took a step back and glanced to Ada.

"This is my daughter, Ada." He squeezed Ada's hand and gestured toward Rachel. "This is one of Erin's sisters. Remember me telling you she had three?"

"I'm Rachel," she said as she extended her hand. "It's so nice to meet you."

Ada shook her hand and smiled. "You're really pretty just like Erin. Do you all look the same?"

Rachel laughed and dropped her hand. "Well, thank you for the compliment. We do all definitely favor each other."

"So how have you been?" he asked, amazed she still looked like the same Rachel he remembered with her dark blond hair in a simple braid over one shoulder and those signature Spencer green eyes.

"Doing great," she replied with a sigh. "Married now and I'm helping my family on the farm with our event space. I also got my degree so I can help other farmers get started off on the right foot."

Joe rocked back on his booted heels. "Impressive, and you sound very busy. I heard how successful the farm-to-table events were."

Gram had told him the old barn had been converted into an event space, which they used to host ticketed dinners that featured food from Four Sisters. The venue could also be rented for special occasions, like the one Erin mentioned they'd hosted on Sunday. The entire family pitched in whenever they could and wherever was needed to make their new business venture a success.

"Beyond anything we'd ever dreamed," she agreed. "All

of that was Jenn's idea, though. I have to give her the credit, even though I'm the go-to for getting things scheduled and finalized."

Jenn, another sister, who had lost her husband years ago and moved away. Joe had heard she'd come back and remarried. Good for her for taking back her life and finding happiness again. Not everyone would be that strong to start completely over, but the Spencer family had always been very close and strong in their faith so this came as no surprise.

"What brings you two out today?" Rachel asked.

"We need some chickens," Ada piped up before Joe could say a word, but he laughed.

"We want to *discuss* chickens," he corrected. "I haven't agreed to anything yet and we need something Gram is on board with because when we leave, she has to care for them."

Ada always came up with crazy ideas and had such a free spirit about her. He tried to tap into all of her interests, but this one required some research before any type of commitment.

"There's a variety of chickens we can get," Rachel supplied. "Just depending on what you want them for, meat or eggs or both, and how many you'd like. You'd need a coop as well and we sell those or you can build one."

"Maybe we could come by your farm and see what you have," Ada added, looking up to Rachel.

"Well, which farm?" Rachel propped her hand on her hip. "I have one with my husband, Jack, and my parents own one. But you're in luck. They are next door to each other so maybe you could come to both."

"Really?" Ada's brows rose as her eyes widened and her head swiveled between Joe and Rachel. "Like today?"

Rachel tipped her head, but Joe intervened. "Let's just wait and see when Rachel has the time, okay?"

"I will actually be at Four Sisters tomorrow morning," Rachel stated. "I'm meeting a client to go over final details of their wedding shower. She's coming about nine. So would you all want to come around ten?"

Ada enthusiastically pumped her fist in the air and shouted, "Yes!"

Rachel laughed and glanced at Joe. "I guess I'll see you then."

"I guess we can discuss all things chickens then, too?" Joe asked. "And I can see what coops you have, but I'm sure you have something larger than we'd ever need."

"We'll get you set up," Rachel assured him. "And make sure Garnet can take care of them once you're gone."

Joe sighed and shook his head. "I don't even know how I got talked into this," he muttered to himself.

"She's pretty adorable and convincing." Rachel glanced at Ada and chuckled. "That's how."

"I like her," his daughter stated. "Are your other sisters like you and Erin?"

Rachel nodded. "Pretty much. We have another sister Violet who is a veterinarian and Jenn who owns a salon in town. She's actually expecting a baby and she has a little girl who is just a little older than you, if I had to guess."

Ada perked up even more. "Really? I need to meet her, too. I only know Willow."

"I got to meet Willow, too," Rachel added. "She's quiet but seems like a sweetheart. It's good you two have each other over the summer."

Ada glanced at Joe. "Can Willow come to the farm, too?"

Joe recalled what Erin had said about Willow getting

upset last time she was there but didn't want to get into that here or step into family issues. Erin was her guardian and would decide if Willow could come.

"I'm sure we can work something out," Rachel replied.

Joe would have to discuss with Erin before any promises were made, but he hoped Willow could overcome her fears or whatever seemed to hold her back last time she'd been at Four Sisters. Joe knew he'd have to reach out to Erin and have a discussion that had nothing to do with tutoring. They hadn't spoken since sitting next to each other in church. They'd attended so many services together as teens, shoulders brushing as they listened to Pastor Matthew's sermons. Which was why he hadn't expected her nearness during service recently to affect him so much. He remembered her kind way when she spoke to others, and the way her face looked so peaceful when she prayed. He hadn't been able to stop thinking about her since.

And at some point they'd have to discuss their past... if nothing else than to bury old feelings once and for all.

"What about just a few lighter pieces to frame your face?" Jenn suggested, sliding her hands through Erin's hair.

Erin stared back at her sister's reflection in the mirror at the salon. "I'd pay you just to keep playing with my hair to be honest. It's more relaxing than anything."

"I know you're stressed." Jenn continued to look through Erin's hair. "But that's why you're here and you're not paying me. We'll do what you want and it's on me."

"Oh, no," Erin insisted. "First of all, this is your business and I'm paying like any other customer. Second, you and Luke have one child and another on the way. You certainly need it."

Jenn patted her swollen belly. "We will be just fine, I promise. And don't get used to this treatment. It's only on the house this time."

Erin laughed. "I'm going to pay you, so don't be ridiculous. But I would let you show me how to style Willow's hair while mine is processing if that's okay?"

Jenn nodded. "Of course. She's got all those beautiful natural curls. It can be a blessing or a curse, but I'll help you."

"I've just been doing ponytails, but she might be getting sick of that."

Jenn glanced to the little waiting area where Willow sat with her little bag of goodies Erin had brought. She currently had her coloring book out, the one with the birthday party theme.

"She's adjusting okay still?" Jenn asked.

Erin pulled in a deep breath. "For the most part, but when I went to the farm the other day, something about Dad really set her off. She got scared and I'm not sure if it's just because he's taller and a bigger guy who looks intimidating or if he reminds her of someone that hurt her."

Jenn's brows drew in. "Dad would never hurt anyone, let alone a child."

"I know that, but she doesn't, so now I have to figure out how to ease her back into the family and onto the farm."

Jenn pursed her lips. "What about showing her some old family photos? When we're all together and Dad is smiling. Maybe if she sees all of us as a happy unit, she'll see there's no threat."

Erin liked that idea and would definitely try doing just that.

"I wondered if maybe Paisley could come over to the house one day," Erin hedged.

She loved seeing her niece, and the eight-year-old hadn't

been introduced to Willow yet. She knew Ada had been a positive influence on Willow and Erin had even considered asking Joe for a playdate outside of tutoring, but it seemed a bit awkward about asking her ex for another reason to hang around.

"Just having another child over who is happy might help," Erin added.

"I will absolutely do that," Jenn promised. "She and Luke went on a run in another county. She can't get enough of watching him work with pregnant animals."

Jenn's husband, Luke, was a large animal vet and mostly traveled to working farms. But he and Jenn also had a piece of land at Four Sisters where they lived and kept an office for his work. When Luke's brother and sister-in-law passed away a couple of years ago, Luke gained sole custody of his niece. Now he and Jenn raised their sweet girl together. They were building a beautiful life and Erin couldn't be happier.

"So, about those lighter pieces?" Jenn circled back to hair and smiled in the mirror. "Can I just do what I think is best?"

Erin nodded. "Sure. You've never steered me wrong before. I trust you."

"I'll go mix the color now."

Jenn turned and practically skipped to the back room. Still grinning, Erin turned in her chair to face where Willow sat coloring.

"Are you excited to get your hair fixed?" she asked.

Willow glanced up and nodded.

"You are allowed to tell my sister if there's something you want done or if there's anything you don't like," Erin told her. "Nobody will be upset. This is your hair and we want you happy. That sound like a plan?"

Again, Willow nodded, then went back to coloring. Erin hoped getting Willow out of the house more and more would also help her come out of the silence she'd been living in. Integrating with society, seeing how people interacted on a positive level, would hopefully only benefit this sweet girl.

Erin's cell vibrated on the vanity top. She reached to see the text message that popped up on the screen and recognized one of her coworkers, Sasha. Well, former coworkers.

She swiped the screen and read the message.

I'm so sorry to bother you with this favor and please tell me no if you're not comfortable with helping...but is there any chance you can help again with the Back to School Bash? You've always spearheaded that and I hate asking, but...

Erin stared at the long text as her heart ached. She had always loved planning the Back to School Bash and all of the festivities that went along with it. Incorporating the town into the evening of fun had been so rewarding. Stations with free haircuts for kids, another one with free school supplies, a game area where students could get to know teachers in a fun way while earning prizes.

She'd been so consumed with getting out her résumé to a variety of schools, both in her county and surrounding areas, taking care of Willow and being thrown for a loop by Joe's commanding presence, she hadn't thought of the event one time.

She stared down at her phone, and the hurt human side of her wanted to decline as nicely as possible. But the teacher and the Christian in her urged her to help because nobody knew this event like she did. She'd been in charge every year and just because she wasn't employed with the district anymore didn't mean she couldn't help. After all, the entire community came out to help, right? She was a community member now.

And she could tell by the text that Sasha felt bad, which made Erin feel bad, too.

She quickly replied.

I would love to keep up this tradition. Don't be sorry for asking. We all want the kids to have the best time. I'll get everything in motion and be in touch soon.

Erin put the cell back on the white and gold vanity and eased back in her seat. She turned to Willow and wondered if this wouldn't be a perfect project for her to help with. She loved art and she wanted to be useful. As much as Erin's heart hurt to not be going back to school with her friends and the new students she would welcome like her own, she still wanted to contribute to a successful year.

Just as Jenn came back through the salon with bowls full of color, Erin's cell vibrated once again.

She fully expected to see another text from her coworker, but Joe's name popped up and an instant tingle of nerves and anticipation replaced all other emotions. Why did she still have these feelings? Were they old ones resurfacing or were they completely new and out of the blue?

Erin swiped the screen and read the message.

Need to talk to you

Her heart kicked up even more now at the ominous message.

"Oh, that looks serious." Jenn peeked over Erin's shoulder. "What does he want?"

Erin shielded the phone against her chest and scoffed. "It's not polite to snoop."

"Then don't keep secrets." Jenn laughed. "How is Joe? I haven't seen him yet. From the looks of that text, you've seen him lots."

Erin glanced at Willow to make sure she was still doing okay. She had pulled out the baggie of cheddar crackers they'd brought for a snack and seemed quite content.

"We've seen each other," Erin confirmed. "Tutoring Ada has been going well so far. But if you're implying anything more is happening, you're wrong. He's leaving at the end of the summer. Our lives and goals are no different than they were ten years ago."

Jenn started dividing her hair and clipping sections out of the way, but she pursed her lips as if in deep thought. Thankfully the salon door chime jingled announcing a new visitor.

"Nobody invited me for girl day?"

Violet closed the door behind her and dropped her purse in the waiting chair next to Willow.

"Hi, sweetie," she greeted the little girl. "Are you getting your hair done, too?"

Willow put another cracker in her mouth and nodded. Violet said nothing else as she pulled the band from her ponytail and shook out her hair and made her way toward the station.

"What are you doing here?" Jenn asked.

"I saw Erin's clunker out front and thought I'd swing by on my way home. No offense," Vi quickly added.

Erin laughed. "None taken. My poor car definitely needs to be replaced, but there's always something else and I don't want to spend the money. Especially now."

She laid her phone in her lap and sighed. Maybe when she found a new job she could start looking at a different car.

"Is that Joe?" Violet asked, looking down at the phone.

Erin didn't even think and had the screen laying face up. She rolled her eyes and flipped the phone down onto her lap.

"You two are like nosy old ladies," Erin grumbled. "Yes, it's Joe. No, nothing is going on. Yes, we've talked. Does that sum everything up?"

Erin watched in the mirror as her sisters exchanged a glance.

"Should we call Rachel here, too, just so you all can quiz me?" Erin added.

"She seems cranky," Vi whispered.

"Apparently Joe is a touchy subject now that they've been talking," Jenn muttered back.

Erin loved her well-meaning sisters, and joking had always been part of their lives. She couldn't say she wouldn't be the same if the roles were reversed and she wasn't the baby of the family. There really weren't many, if any, secrets between them.

Once again, her cell vibrated and she was afraid to look with her sisters standing right over her. She carefully turned her phone to see the screen. A message from her sister Rachel popped up.

Joe and Ada stopped into the feedstore earlier and she asked about checking out the farm. I said I could meet them tomorrow at 10, but something came up. Can you meet with them?

Ada had asked about going to the farm? Why hadn't Joe just come straight to Erin to ask? Was he afraid she'd say no?

"Problem?" Vi asked.

Erin shook her head. "No, but I can't believe you didn't look."

"Oh, I did. I just didn't know if it was a problem," Violet replied with a shrug.

Jenn let out a snicker as she pulled the foil sheets from her cart.

"Of course you snooped," Erin muttered. "And no, there's no problem. I'm not afraid of being around Joe."

Yet, since sitting with him at church, she couldn't deny she was more drawn to him than she should be. But she couldn't help her feelings or what direction her heart moved in. She just couldn't act on it.

Her sisters exchanged knowing glances in the mirror and Erin let out another sigh.

"Just say it," she told them. "Whatever you're thinking, just let it out."

"I'm just wondering if you're telling us that you've moved on or telling yourself," Jenn supplied. "Nothing to be ashamed of if you still have a thing for Joe."

"Have a thing?" Erin snorted. "I'm not sixteen. I'm a twenty-eight-year-old woman."

"Whose one true love left town and is back after ten years," Violet reminded her. "You can't tell me old feelings haven't been stirred."

Oh, they were stirred, but that wasn't anything she was about to share with her meddling yet well-meaning sisters.

Without a word, she sent a text back to Rachel that she would meet Joe and Ada at the farm. Now she just had to make sure her father kept his distance so Willow felt safe. She knew Willow would love the animals and her time with Ada, so if she focused on that aspect and hyped it up, hopefully this visit would go a bit more smoothly than the last one.

And no doubt her sisters would either want a follow-up to the day's outing or they'd just show up to spy in person.

Regardless, she would be spending quality time with Joe and their little girls and Erin couldn't ignore that lump in her throat. The image of all of them on a farm mimicked the dream she'd had so long ago. But this was the reality she lived in and she wasn't doing herself, or anyone else, any good by getting swept up in the past or in what might have been.

Chapter Eight

Joe steered his rental down the drive to Four Sisters and made his way beneath the old metal arch. He hadn't been on this property in over a decade and somehow he'd just gone back in time. Not much had changed. The white fencing still ran parallel up either side of the drive leading to the old two-story farmhouse. The large oak trees stood proud and tall and the tire swing still swayed in the breeze. There was a new home at the front of the property and he'd heard that belonged to Jenn and her new husband, Luke.

"This is just like I thought it would be," Ada stated from the back seat as she pressed her hands against the glass with her little face between them. "Just like the shows we watched. All this green grass and the animals are different from back home, and that house is huge."

Joe chuckled. He assumed the size of an old farmhouse would look huge to a little girl who only lived in a two-bedroom home not even one thousand square feet. And Gram's house was just a small cottage as well, but he'd never thought of the place capturing Ada's attention.

"It's a beautiful place," he agreed as he pulled up near the main barn. At least, he assumed this was still the main one they kept their horses in.

"Do you see Rachel?" Ada asked.

He glanced around but didn't. He did however see Erin's little yellow car. He didn't know Erin would be here, though Rachel had mentioned working something out. And perhaps Erin was trying to fix that wedge between Will and Willow. He hoped so because from what he could tell, that shy girl needed all the love she deserved. The Spencer family were some of the most kind, caring people he'd ever known and he'd met thousands of people over his ten years and two continents of ministry.

Ada let out a little squeal the moment she stepped from the car. "Is Willow going to be here? I didn't know that."

Yeah, he hadn't known, either. But this was Erin's parents' house, so it wasn't out of the ordinary for her and Willow to be here.

He glanced around the old homestead, thinking of all the time he'd spent here with Erin and her sisters when he was in high school. He hadn't expected so much nostalgia to hit him when he came back. Why did he feel he had one foot in Rosewood Valley and one in Senegal? His heart was torn. He wanted to return to Senegal and the huge opportunity waiting for him there. But the idea of staying longer in his hometown, spending time with Gram and at his old church, appealed to him more than he wanted to admit. He'd assumed this would be a nice summer visit and at the end of his time he'd return to the life he'd created.

What about the life he'd created here? At church and in this community? The life that shaped him and made him the man he was today.

"I thought I heard a car pull in."

Joe turned to see Erin stepping out of the open door of the barn. Willow was right at her side and the image of this cowgirl and her little girl, both wearing adorable hats, had his heart clenching. This trip had been reminding him of everything he'd given up when he left. The farm, the family…the girl.

"You *are* here!" Ada exclaimed as she raced toward Willow. "This day is even better."

Ada hugged Willow and Willow wrapped her arms around her new friend. This was the first sign of emotion he'd seen from her and from the look on Erin's face, she was just as happy and surprised as he was. Erin's genuine smile lit up her entire face as she stared at the scene next to her. Obviously a child closer to her own age put Willow at ease, as opposed to adults who left her nervous. Although, Willow had seemed relaxed the more she'd greeted church-goers last Sunday. Perhaps that had helped.

Whatever she was doing with her foster child seemed to be working and moving in a positive direction—not that he had any doubt.

"I hope it's okay that I'm meeting you," Erin told him as she brought her green eyes to meet his. "Rachel texted me that she wasn't able to, so I thought this would be a great time to show Willow around the farm and let her see the animals as well."

He'd be lying if he said he wasn't happier seeing Erin than Rachel. Oh, the oldest Spencer sister was perfectly fine, but nobody was Erin. Nobody.

"I'm good with that," he told her casually, then leaned in and lowered his voice. "Did things get squared away with your dad and Willow?"

Erin pulled in a deep breath. "Not really. I promised her a day of fun and said that while my dad is the kindest man, I understood her fear and she would not have to see him. I gave her the option and she truly wanted to see the animals."

Joe shifted his body so the girls couldn't see his face. "Did she say why he scared her?"

Erin shook her head. "I think this is just another hurdle she has to overcome with the proper help and care. She'll be fine. She was apprehensive about coming, but once I promised animals and Ada, she perked up. I told her my dad would be too busy to come around and I just gave him a heads-up that we'd be taking some horses out into the east pasture."

Joe nodded. "Sounds good. I wasn't sure what all we'd get into. I guess I should've brought a hat."

He tapped the tip of her brown rim. "You still have the same one."

She shrugged and smiled. "I've bought others over the years, but this one is familiar and I can't let it go."

This was how he remembered her. When he'd been in Africa and she'd cross his mind, this was the exact image he got. Simple button-up shirt, worn jeans, dusty cowgirl boots, this light brown hat with the thin black band around the perimeter.

"I have an extra one in here for you," she told him. "I bought Willow and Ada one last night when Rachel texted me. Just something fun for them."

She'd bought the girls their own hats? But of course she had. That teacher in her wanted kids to feel included and special. She had a way of making everyone feel that way, and he was no different. He didn't know why his heart seemed to pump faster and his nerves were all a mess or why he couldn't stop smiling like some lovestruck teen.

This visit was temporary and there was certainly no room for the what-ifs or what-could-have-been moments.

"Did you hear that?" Joe asked as he turned to Ada. "Erin got you a hat to wear today."

"Actually I let Willow pick it out," Erin chimed in. "Come on into the barn and I'll introduce you all to the horses."

The moment they stepped into the barn, another wave of memories slid to the forefront of his mind. That familiar smell of straw and wood. The scuffle of hooves on the concrete and the snorts to get your attention. He'd missed this lifestyle more than he thought.

"Ada, if you're comfortable riding a horse on your own, we have a very gentle one perfect for you," Erin told her. "Willow isn't quite ready yet, so she'll be riding with me."

"I want to do it myself." Ada stopped in front of a stall and clapped her hands. "This one. What's his name?"

Erin laughed. "That's a mare, which means female. Her name is Sunshine. And that is the exact one you will be riding. She's a total sweetheart."

The girls stepped closer to Erin as she reached up and ran her hand down Sunshine's nose. Joe stood back as Erin went into full teacher mode going over the safety rules for being around horses and riding. She explained how this was going to be so fun, but they always had to be careful. He hadn't ridden a horse since he left, but he hadn't forgotten a thing. You couldn't grow up in Rosewood Valley and not be accustomed to horses and farm life. Even though his Gram lived in town in a small cottage, Joe had always had friends with farms, and then Erin had come into his life and he'd spent a good amount of time at Four Sisters.

"First order of business for a cowgirl is to get the hat," Erin stated.

She moved down the aisle between the stalls and stepped into the small tack room where all the supplies were stored. Moments later she came back out with two hats, one large black one and one small purple one.

"Here you go." She beamed as she handed over the accessories to Joe and Ada. "You need the full experience."

"Oh, I remember everything," Joe chuckled. "Especially when Midnight tried to buck me off."

Erin waved a hand to dismiss his statement as she snickered. "You two just had personalities that didn't mesh. Unfortunately, Midnight passed away a few years ago. I think you're good to go with Clover. He's a gentle giant."

The scuff of footsteps behind him had Joe turning around. Sarah Spencer stepped into the barn with the morning sunshine illuminating her. Joe hadn't seen her in so long, but she looked the same, like happiness and warmth. She always had a smile on her face and light in her eyes. Her short hair framed her face and had gotten a bit grayer than he recalled, but other than that Sarah still had that motherly presence that instantly seemed to calm people.

"Good morning," she greeted as she stepped up to them and looked to Ada. "My name is Sarah. I'm Erin's mom."

Ada immediately reached out her hand. "I'm Ada. Your place is so cool. I love all your horses."

Sarah shook Ada's hand and nodded. "Well, thank you. We love it here."

Then she turned to Joe and opened her arms. He wrapped his arms around her petite frame and patted her back. Just like the rest of the Spencer family he'd encountered so far, Sarah acted like no time had passed since he'd last been home.

"You've gotten bigger." Sarah laughed as she eased back. "That didn't come out right. I just mean you're all man now and you were just a teen when you left."

Joe patted her slender shoulders. "No offense taken. I definitely am not the same as when I left."

"It's so good to have you back and I bet Garnet is just loving having you and Ada here."

Joe dropped his hands and took a step back. "She is. She keeps wanting to cook and bake for us, but Ada and I made her take a load off the other day and we pampered her."

"Good for you," Sarah praised, then turned to face Ada and Willow. "I know you're getting ready to go for a ride, but I wanted to see if you two young ladies could help me in the kitchen afterward. I have the farmers market coming up this weekend and could use some help with labeling all my jars."

Willow shifted her attention to Erin, but Sarah went on.

"Will is out of town for the day," she explained. "He had to help a friend at his ranch so I'm a bit shorthanded."

"I want to help," Ada chimed in. "Willow, will you come with me?"

Willow looked to her new friend and after a brief pause she ultimately nodded. "Yes."

A confirmation *and* speaking. This girl was moving right along.

"Wonderful." Sarah clasped her hands together. "And for your work, I might have a special treat for you ladies."

"Then we better get started riding so they can get back," Erin said. She faced her mother. "I'll send them in as soon as we're done."

"You guys have fun," Sarah told them as she turned to leave. "It's a beautiful day to spend on the farm."

"Okay, let me get the horses ready and Joe—" she glanced at him "—can help me lead them out. Then we'll get going."

Joe couldn't help but feel a zing of excitement at the way her gaze had connected with his just now, so open and trusting. They were doing something special…making a memory together for their little girls. He couldn't wait to get back on a horse for some refreshing, back-to-basics quality time. Now he just had to remember that Erin was only a friend and doing this as a favor to his daughter. Nothing romantic and no spark of old feelings could creep up. Not when the future was so uncertain.

He just had to keep telling himself that until he believed it.

Chapter Nine

Why was she so nervous?

Erin gripped the reins a bit tighter as she secured Willow in front of her. She led the way from the pasture and in the opposite direction from the pond, which was the prettiest spot on the property in her opinion. This rise, where you could see a good bit of land and the house in the distance, always took her breath away.

"Having fun?" she leaned around to ask Willow.

The little girl nodded and turned slightly with a smile on her face.

Joe rode up beside her with Ada next to him.

"Hard to deny the goodness of God when you can see all this beauty." She sighed, taking in the sight.

"I agree." His voice slid over the breeze with a rough murmur.

She glanced to Joe and noticed he wasn't looking at the scenery at all, but directly at her. All thoughts vanished, her heart clenched, and her words caught in her throat. What could she even say to that statement?

Her eyes held his for longer than she should allow, but she couldn't look away. The fine lines around his mouth were signs he'd been smiling and laughing over the years. That validation warmed her. No matter how shattered her heart was at that time, and for a good bit after, she wanted nothing but to see him happy.

But the way he was looking at her now didn't seem joyous, but rather...sad. She couldn't quite pinpoint that emotion reflecting in his dark eyes. Something was bothering him.

"Can we get a horse for back home?"

Ada's question cut through the moment and pulled Joe's gaze away. Erin inhaled deeply and focused her attention on the little girl staring at her father for an answer.

"I want to show my friends I can ride," she went on.

"I'm not sure we have a space to house a horse or care for it properly," Joe replied. "But we can see about getting a pet if that would be a good compromise."

"I'll hold out for a horse," she insisted. "Just like this one."

Joe shot Erin a look that said he'd tried but wasn't pressing the issue. Erin merely shrugged as she clenched the reins once more.

"Let's head on back," she suggested. "I'm sure Mom has the entire kitchen lined with unlabeled jars just waiting on her helpers." She grinned at Ada before turning her mare away.

They rode the rest of the way back in silence, which was perfect because she needed a little breather from the intensity of Joe's bold statement, quickly followed by that heavy-lidded stare. What had he been thinking? Had the girls not been around, would he have said more?

She couldn't get her hopes up that something would start brewing between them again. Just because her sisters had all recently found happiness and started their familial journey in whatever manner worked for them, didn't mean this was Erin's time. The odds were certainly against her that she and Joe would or could rekindle any sort of romance.

But she had to be honest with herself that she would likely always have feelings for Joe. How could she not? He was her first love…her only love, if she were being honest.

They pulled up to the back door and Erin slid off the saddle, then reached up to help Willow down. Joe assisted Ada and both girls went to the steps just as Erin's mom opened the back door. She had on her signature yellow apron Erin had made her years ago. Tradition was a staple here in the Spencer household.

"You girls are just in time," Sarah Spencer declared. "Fresh chocolate chip cookies just came out of the oven."

"Can we have those before we work?" Ada asked.

"Ada," Joe warned.

Erin's mom laughed. "I think after riding you've probably earned a little snack and warm cookies are the best kind."

Willow looked back at Erin. "Go on," Erin urged with a smile. "You don't want to miss out on my mom's cookies."

A soft smile flirted around Willow's mouth and Ada took her hand and pulled her inside. Erin couldn't be more thankful for Ada right now. Ada was a bit older, and Erin sensed that Willow had found someone to look up to in her new friend. A child role model would be completely different than an adult, and Willow needed both in her life right now.

"We'll get the horses in their stalls and everything put away," Erin told her mother, who was still holding the door open. "Then I want some cookies for myself."

"I might have to grab at least one as well, Miss Sarah," Joe added. "You know I can't resist anything coming out of your kitchen."

Sarah's grin spread across her face. "I already have some set aside for you to take home for Garnet and Dottie. Don't you worry. And I'll have to have you and Ada over for dinner one night before you leave town. Just as soon as my schedule calms a bit."

"That's an invitation I can't turn down," Joe replied.

Sarah followed the girls on into the house, leaving Joe and Erin with the horses. Erin slid her foot back into the stirrup and palmed the horn as she hoisted herself back into the saddle.

"I can lead Sunshine if you want to follow," she told him.

As she circled around Joe's horse, he handed up the lead to Sunshine. Without a word, he fell in behind on his own horse and they went back toward the barn. Nothing but birds chirping and warm sunshine enveloped them. Well, a good dose of tension, at least on her side. She was keenly aware of Joe trailing just behind her as they approached the empty barn. She wasn't sure how to proceed without the cushion of little girls. That was the new tie that bound them together.

Erin wasn't so sure she wanted to rely on the old binding tie to fall back on. It would be all too easy to slip back into that mindset of a lovestruck teenager. She couldn't slip back there, though. Yes, they shared a connection that time couldn't erase, but they had responsibilities now and more to worry about than attraction.

They entered the dimly lit outbuilding and dismounted. Just like years ago, Erin and Joe worked together getting the saddles and blankets put back into the tack room. She hung Sunshine's saddle in its usual spot, and when she turned, there he was with the reins and bits. She started to reach for them when he finally broke the silence.

"Thanks for letting Ada come out today."

Erin nodded. "Of course. But she asked Rachel, not me, so you can tell Rachel." She smiled.

Joe's lips quivered in a half grin. "Yeah, about that—"

"You put a child up to asking?" she joked. "Really, Joe. I would think you'd be more mature than that."

That familiar grin deepened the fine lines around his mouth and Erin's butterflies tingled in her stomach with attraction. Still, after all these years, just one simple look had the ability to give her those teen crush feelings all over again.

"She wanted me to ask and I had every intention," he assured her. "Then we ran into Rachel and when I introduced her as your sister, Ada jumped at the chance to see the animals."

Erin reached for the reins he held, taking them carefully so their fingers didn't brush. "You're good," she told him. "I just like giving you a hard time."

She hung them up and when she faced him again, he hadn't moved. And that intense stare was back. She wasn't sure what he was thinking but she couldn't keep doing this. He was standing so close.

"Joe."

He took a half step forward.

"This…"

"I know," he murmured, his gaze never wavering. "I didn't expect all these emotions to creep back up."

Erin swallowed as he took another half step forward. He was very close now. If he reached for her, Erin wasn't sure she'd have the willpower to resist.

"You're not staying," she reminded him. "Any old feelings have no purpose here. I don't… I *can't* get hurt again."

His hand froze midair. A muscle clenched in his jaw and those lids lowered just enough to shield the pain in his eyes, which she caught just seconds before his gaze shuddered. He pulled in a deep breath.

Then his warm hand cupped her cheek and Erin instinctively turned into his touch. That strong hand, the familiar caress, had her closing her eyes, and she didn't know if she was caught up in the nostalgia of their past or trying to capture a brand-new moment.

But why? What would relishing in this instant do? No good could come from this. She had to focus on Willow and finding a job, not reconnecting with her ex.

"Joe." The word came out on a whisper as she opened her eyes.

"I had no intention of hurting you," he murmured. "Not then and certainly not now. I'm amazed at the woman you've become and I just…"

She stared into those dark eyes and waited for him to finish, but the silence and the weight of all the unspoken words settled heavy between them.

"What?" she couldn't help but ask.

His lips thinned for a fraction of a second before he replied, "I just never expected how hard I'd be pulled back in."

A statement she not only understood but felt to her very core. She'd been given the heads-up about him coming back to town, but there was no mental preparation that could have gotten her ready for the reality of seeing Joe face-to-face again. Not only that, but helping his daughter, knowing he even *had* a daughter and now the powerful stares and delicate touches.

"I don't know what you want me to say," she admitted honestly. "We both have different lives. I'm here, you're there. Nothing has changed in ten years except now you're a father and I'm a foster mom."

That muscle ticked in his jaw again as if frustration had settled in. Well, join the club. She didn't like this one bit, either.

"How is this even possible?" she added. "So much time and distance between us and yet, there's still…something."

His other hand came up and now he framed her face as that penetrating stare held her in place. He had the most gentle touch for someone with such a commanding presence. He'd always been a tender leader, someone who was soft yet powerful. He had the perfect mix of traits that made him an amazing missionary.

She just wished he hadn't been called to lead so far away. But wishes wouldn't change the past or the present.

"It never went away," he murmured as his gaze dropped to her lips. "I didn't know that until now."

He leaned in, ever so slowly, as if giving her the opportunity to stop this madness. She had no resolve where he was concerned. Not only that, part of her wondered if everything was indeed the same. Would a kiss remind her of all that they'd had? All that she'd lost? Or would she realize once and for all that this relationship was over?

Erin curled her fingers around his shoulders and met him halfway. The second his lips brushed hers, she knew for a fact what they'd shared was not over. The familiarity, the warmth, the tenderness only reminded her of how amazing they'd been together.

He felt like home. He always had and now she knew for a fact that those feelings weren't adolescent or naive. He'd grown into the man she'd always imagined. A strong leader, firm in his faith, and a protective, loving father. How could she not be falling for him more now than before?

The way he tipped her head, still holding her gently, had her sighing and leaning into him just a bit more. This was absolutely crazy and one, if not both, of them was going to get hurt. He'd been in town less than a week and already she was kissing him. Or he was kissing her. She really wasn't sure at this point and she was too enamored by the man and the moment to analyze it any further. She couldn't get entangled with him again. The scuff of a boot on the concrete had her jerking away. Joe's broad build blocked her view of the door, but Erin leaned around to find her sister Violet standing there with wide eyes. Not just Violet, but Violet's soon-to-be sister-in-law, Clara. When did she get into town?

Erin felt like she was a teen getting caught doing something she shouldn't be doing, which was ridiculous. She and Joe were grown adults. So what, they'd shared a kiss.

"We can come back," Violet finally said, then smiled when Joe turned to face her.

"No need." Joe's calming voice coupled with his easy grin irked Erin. How could he be so blasé about this? Her nerves were a jumbled mess and she couldn't stop this insistent out-of-control feeling.

"Our girls are just inside helping your mother put labels on her jars," Joe went on. "We should go check on them, anyway."

Then as if he remembered his manners, he moved toward the opening of the door and extended his hand toward Clara. "I'm Joe," he introduced.

The tall blonde shook his hand and smiled. "I'm Clara. Vi is marrying my brother." Vi was engaged to the new town sheriff, Dax Adams, and had since become close with his twin sister. "I'm just in visiting from Oregon and being nosy with the farm. Four Sisters makes me want to move here and start my own ranch."

"Then that's what you should do," Joe replied. "Don't let doubts get in the way of dreams."

"That's great advice," she told him.

Joe glanced over his shoulder to Erin. "Ready to go inside?"

Was she ready to go anywhere with him? No. She needed a moment to gather her thoughts and compose herself, but at the same time she didn't want Joe to walk away and leave her with her sister who would no doubt start asking questions that Erin didn't have the answers to.

"Ready," she said as she headed to the door. "Clara, it's great to have you back in town and you can come here anytime."

Erin tossed her sister a glance and Violet merely raised her brows, the silent gesture that they would be talking later. Lovely. Erin couldn't wait because by the time she and Vi got to discuss what had just happened, both Rachel and Jenn would know.

The last thing she needed was all her happily married or almost married sisters getting involved in something Erin didn't even understand herself. There would be no way to go through an inquisition with those three. Right now, though, Erin needed to focus on Joe and try to come to some sort of understanding on what that kiss meant... or didn't mean.

Chapter Ten

"**P**erfect."

Sarah praised the girls as she glanced over to the jars they had labeled. Joe and Erin had come into the kitchen to check on the girls after they'd been caught in the barn. He still couldn't believe he'd kissed her, but the other side of him couldn't believe it took him this long to just give in to what he'd been fighting since he returned.

"I think you two are doing a fabulous job," Erin added. "Mom might make you guys permanent helpers."

"I just might at that," Sarah agreed. "They work so well together. They remind me of when I had you and your sisters in here. The giggles and the chatter is just what my kitchen was missing."

This was the second time in as many days that Willow and Ada had been referred to or hinted at as sisters. He absolutely loved their relationship and couldn't be happier that Ada had found someone she wanted to spend time with this summer.

"I want to do this all the time." Willow jumped up from her seat and went to get another sheet of stickers to label. "And I'm learning everything about jelly. I want to try them all."

Erin laughed and her face lit up radiantly. Joe grit his

teeth, trying to focus on the happiness of the moment and not how he kept replaying that kiss over and over in his mind. Erin's laugh was still so sweet and exactly how he remembered. So was that kiss.

He shouldn't have done it. What purpose did kissing her serve? Now all he'd do was wonder if he'd pulled them both over a line they couldn't step back over... And what was Erin thinking? Had that private moment affected her the same way?

"I think I can manage to send a couple jars of jelly home with each of you if you'd like to pick out two that sound the best," Sarah promised, eyeing the girls.

"I can pay you for them," Joe interjected. "I know this is your business."

"Oh, please." Sarah waved him off. "I am happy to give my helpers a little gift." She picked up some of the labeled jars and put them on the kitchen island before turning back to the table. "Same goes for you, Willow. Find two flavors you'd like to take with you."

Willow's face lit up and Joe was starting to see more and more of the little girl inside her shell come out. Of course Erin was to be commended for the love, care, and attention she devoted to Willow. Even in the midst of her own worries and stress from being let go from a job she loved, she still managed to put her own needs aside for the good of others.

And that was just the type of woman she was, the same woman he remembered. She'd grown so much, yet many things were still the same.

"Dad," came Ada's voice.

Joe blinked and glanced at his daughter. "I'm sorry, what?"

"I asked if you'd like the blueberry or the raspberry," she said with a sigh, clearly not the first time she'd asked.

"Blueberry," he said, "but Sarah doesn't make any bad jellies so you can't go wrong."

"I think Gram One and Gram Two will like raspberry so I'll get that."

Sarah laughed. "Is that Garnet and Dottie?" she asked.

Joe nodded. "She didn't know what to call Dottie and thought that was easiest and both of them love it, so there you have it."

"That is just adorable," Erin declared with a little sigh. "How precious that you have two grandmothers to visit you right now."

"They went shopping today," Ada added. "But when they get back, Gram Two said she wants to show me how to do puzzles."

Willow smiled but looked back to the labels.

"Can Willow come over, too, Dad?"

Joe nodded. "Of course. She's welcome anytime she wants."

"And Erin?"

Joe glanced at Erin whose eyes had widened at the innocent request. So she wasn't as unaffected as she seemed to be letting on. Part of him was glad their shared kiss had made an impact, but the other part of him worried this would complicate things even more.

"Erin and Willow are always welcome," he stated, still keeping his eyes locked on Erin.

He meant every word because he couldn't just start ignoring her because he feared where that kiss would lead them. All he could do was make some sort of attempt to get control over his emotions because now there wasn't just he and Erin; they both had girls thrown into the mix.

"Amen."

Joe concluded the prayer and looked out over the congregation. Many faces he recognized, some he didn't. The church had grown since he'd left town and that was such a blessing to see.

Multiple times he saw his Gram and Dottie nodding in agreement with words he shared. Just those little gestures helped boost him and gave him the confidence that he was going in the right direction with this message.

He exhaled and dismissed the crowd after concluding his first sermon at his home church. He'd preached around the globe during his work as a missionary, but he couldn't recall a more important place or time in his life to spread the word of God than his hometown. He kept his sermon on the subject of coming home and how it was never too late to start fresh or make amends. While homecoming was his theme for the summer, he wanted everyone in the congregation to understand it was never too late to return where their roots were or to ask for a second chance. Wasn't that what faith was supposed to do? Always allow for those second chances.

And he couldn't help but wonder if he was indeed preaching to himself.

Joe smiled at the cutest little face sitting in the front row. Ada hadn't taken her eyes off him, but that's how she always was. She came with him everywhere and he was just thankful she loved her faith. He had a good feeling God would call her to something special when the time came.

There were other faces in the crowd that also made him smile…like the entire Spencer clan. Joe hadn't met the new ones, like Jenn's husband and little girl or Rachel's husband. He had run into Sheriff Adams at the coffee shop the other morning and knew he was engaged to Violet. He missed how this small ranch town ticked—it wasn't hard to learn everyone's business, but it wasn't hard to find a helping hand or an act of kindness, either. There were so many things and people to catch up on, he didn't think he could consume it all by the time summer was over. His heart twinged a little at the thought of leaving.

And then, of course, there was Erin. She'd kept her eyes locked on his the entire time as well. He'd tried his hardest not to focus on her or get distracted. The woman had done nothing but be distracting since he'd gotten into town.

And that kiss...

Two days ago they'd shared an intimate moment in her parents' barn, and he'd been reminded of them as teens sneaking a kiss or two in private. Now they were acting the same because getting caught by Violet had obviously shaken up Erin. They hadn't had a chance to talk privately since that day.

Now, not only was the giant question mark surrounding that kiss hovering over them, but they had this wedge of confusion that two days of not speaking to each other had filled.

Joe stepped down from the pulpit and was immediately approached by Will Spencer.

"Wonderful message," Will stated as he reached to shake Joe's hand. "It's good to have you back in town and you've really grown into quite the young man."

Joe shook his hand and couldn't help but be filled with a sense of pride. "Thank you," he replied. "That means a great deal coming from you."

Will dropped his hand and adjusted his tan suit jacket. "I'm sorry I missed seeing you the other day. I had some business to attend to and I promised Erin I'd steer clear until her little one wasn't so afraid anymore. Apparently the social worker told Erin I remind Willow of one of her father's friends who wasn't nice."

"Hopefully she will come around," Joe agreed.

Before he could say more, Sharma Townsend, the head of town council, came up and inserted herself between them. With her bold attitude, flashy jewelry, and bright clothing, Joe nearly laughed. She hadn't changed one bit. She was a bit older than him, but they'd always attended the same church when he lived here and she'd had a tenacity for sparkly and over-the-top everything. Some things never change.

"Good morning, Mrs. Townsend," Joe greeted.

Will waved goodbye from behind her and Joe merely nodded.

"That was so refreshing and wonderful," Sharma praised.

Her bright pink lipstick matched her long dress perfectly and her blue, green, and pink jewelry looked like something his daughter would love.

"I appreciate that," replied with a smile. "It's so nice to see you again. You're as beautiful as I remember."

"Oh, you always were a charmer." She laughed. "Your Gram has just praised you up and down since you left town. That is one proud woman and I can't blame her. The work you're doing in Western Africa and the way you preach, well—" she leaned closer "—I do love Pastor Matthew, but I wouldn't be opposed if you did more preaching while you were in town."

She glanced around, then lowered her voice. "I heard he was thinking of retiring. Not sure if you've thought of staying or not, but you looked right at home up there today."

Right at home. Yeah, he'd felt at home, but didn't want to tap into that further right now. He hadn't come back with any intention of staying. That thought hadn't crossed his mind when he'd decided to make this trip. But the second that seed had been planted, he'd thought of little else.

"I'm glad you enjoyed the sermon," he stated, not divulging any other information. "If you'll excuse me."

He eased aside as Ada came toward him. He scanned the crowd, and he'd be lying to himself if he didn't admit he wanted another glimpse of Erin. She and Willow had sat on the opposite side as her family—Joe had to assume this was because of Will. Joe prayed she'd come to see how caring the older man was. He could be a bit stern-looking, but Joe was sure that Will Spencer would be a doting grandfather to any child who'd let him.

"You did really good." Ada's little hand slid into his as she stared up at him. "I heard some people whispering around me that they thought you should be the new pastor here. Even Gram One and Gram Two were whispering how good you were doing."

Joe had no idea what to say, but this was certainly not a topic he wanted to get into in the middle of a crowd.

"Are we staying here?" she asked, oblivious to his worries. "Because I told Ayonna I'd be back and she could teach me that new game with the balloons."

Exactly. This was the wake-up call he needed. This was the reality he lived in with his daughter who only saw this trip as a vacation. This trip was never supposed to be a potential trial run for relocating. Despite the fact that the job he'd been offered here—which provided fair pay and housing and proximity to family—wasn't something he could write off without thinking it through carefully. Of course Ada would be thinking about her school friends and looking forward to returning home. And at the end of the day he needed to make the decision that was best for his young daughter.

"Let's not worry about this right now," he told her. "How

about we go take the Grams to lunch? I know the perfect place."

Ada's face lit up and she nodded. Joe released the sigh he'd been holding. Why had he not been able to just tell her she'd be back to play that game? Why didn't he confidently believe going back to Africa was their only way?

Those should've been his first thoughts and he should've given reassurances, yet he froze because he hadn't wanted to lie. And he certainly didn't want to have to go back on his word.

Joe started to lead Ada toward the front of the church to find Garnet and Dottie, but he got stopped more times than he could count and the theme of the brief conversations seemed to be the same. The churchgoers had all enjoyed Joe's sermon and wanted more.

And many of them asked if he planned to move back for good, which only heightened his nerves and poured water on those seeds of doubt that had been planted.

"And that cat ended up being the best one we ever had."

Erin sat the picture down on top of the others and shifted on the floral sofa to face Willow. They'd gone through all the pictures Erin had from her childhood, mostly the ones with her father in them so Willow could get a better sense of the man Will Spencer actually was.

"Your dad likes cats?" Willow asked, her eyes still fixed on the image.

Erin nodded, thankful for the full sentence that came from that little mouth. She must really be wondering more if she had that much to say.

"My father loves all animals," Erin replied. "That's why he stays so busy on the farm. He's not only taking care of our land, but also all those animals. I think that's one reason my sister Violet became a veterinarian. We just grew up loving on so many animals and we would have vets come often to help. Violet also runs an animal shelter to help pets find new homes."

Willow leaned back against the arm of the sofa and faced Erin. She stretched her little legs out between them and toyed with the fringe on the pale yellow throw pillow. The way her beautiful doe eyes held Erin's made Erin want to continue. Clearly Willow wanted to know more and was caught up in the Spencer family backstory. But Erin wanted to stay focused on her father so they could all hopefully have a nice family gathering one day.

"My dad never could turn away a stray," Erin added. "That man loves all God's creatures."

Willow pursed her lips together as her eyes darted to her lap, then back up. "So he's always been nice?"

Erin nodded. "I don't know of a kinder man. He can sometimes look scary because he's so tall and broad, so I understand why you were hesitant. You're allowed to feel any way you want. I hope you know that. You won't be punished for being honest with your feelings."

Willow's tiny chin quivered as her eyes filled. "I wanted a nice daddy."

Erin's heart broke at those whispered words, and she eased closer to Willow. "You deserve a nice daddy and a nice mommy. And all my family wants to do is love you. You can be yourself and we will love you no matter what."

A lone tear slid down her cheek and Erin lifted Willow's legs and moved in even closer, until the little girl climbed onto Erin's lap. She rested her head on Erin's shoulder and sniffled.

"This is scary," Willow murmured.

Instinctively Erin wrapped her arms around the girl to hold

her tighter, a silent gesture of reassurance and stability…two factors sorely missing from Willow's life.

"Can I tell you a secret?" Erin asked. When Willow nodded against her shoulder, Erin went on. "I'm scared, too. I've never been a mommy before. And I know I'm not your mommy, but you are the first person I've taken care of outside of my classroom."

Willow lifted her head slightly to meet Erin's gaze.

"I know how to teach kids to spell big words and do fun science projects," Erin continued. "But to care for someone and have them depend on me is a little scary and I don't want to mess up. I want to make sure you're happy and that you love it here. I don't want you to worry about anything as long as you're with me."

Willow rested her head back on Erin's shoulder. "I want to stay."

Erin thought for sure she'd heard her wrong, but she didn't know what else Willow could've said. Did the sweet girl actually want to stay here? Was she afraid to go back to her father? If she had been constantly told to shut up and nobody paid attention to her, it was no wonder she wanted to stay. But Erin could only pray the system did right by Willow…and every other kid. Unfortunately the laws were usually on the side of the parents, and sometimes that was a wonderful thing, while other times it was not.

Erin couldn't exactly voice her opinion to a little girl who was already carrying the weight of her little world on her slender shoulders. This was definitely something to address with the social worker, though. Beth was really trying to make sure the loss of Erin's job didn't upset Willow's placement, and Erin had been diligently working on sending out her résumé. Erin wanted nothing more than to have Willow stay where she was thriving and so deeply loved.

"I'm happy to hear you talking more," Erin admitted, knowing honesty and communication were the key to any type of relationship. "I want to know what you're thinking and feeling. So if you're afraid to talk too much when we're out, you can always share anything here at the house. This is our space, okay?"

Willow nodded again with another sniff. Erin held her tighter, wanting desperately to freeze this moment as a core memory for Willow. One of love and safety. Erin had also incorporated bedtime prayers, hoping Willow would seek solace in the One who could make this situation better. Erin didn't want to think about Willow leaving and going back to her father, but if that day came, Erin hoped prayer was something else Willow took with her.

The cell on the coffee table vibrated and Sarah Spencer's name lit up the screen with a text message.

"Is it okay if I see what my mom needs?" she asked, not wanting Willow to think anything was more important than this moment.

Willow nodded her head, so Erin leaned forward while keeping the little bundle on her lap in a tight hug. When Erin tapped on the message and read, she couldn't help but smile.

"Well, it seems you and Ada made quite an impression on my mom and she wants the two of you to help her at the farmers market tomorrow."

Erin wasn't sure how that would be perceived, but Willow lifted her head, her eyes wide. Considering the seven-year-old had probably never even been to the market in the town park, Erin went on to explain.

"So there's a cute outside shopping area in the park," she started. "And all sorts of people set up tables and sell a variety of things. There's fruits and vegetables, baked goods, homemade purses, and paintings. It's a really neat area. My mom will be selling those jars you guys labeled. She will also have fresh breads and pies. My sisters and I always helped when we were little."

Willow glanced away as if contemplating and Erin figured this might be an overwhelming experience for her, but Erin also knew the market was a safe environment that would be a good experience for both Willow and Ada.

"You know what?" Erin added. "I think this would be a great time for you to also help Ada with math. Money is math problems, right?"

Willow nodded with a soft smile, clearly warming up to the idea.

"So should I tell my mom you'll help? I'll be there, too, if you'd like."

Willow's smile widened as she ultimately nodded and murmured, "Okay."

This was a huge win and step in the right direction. Now if Erin could get her own life, both personal and professional, headed in the same positive direction, she'd be all set.

Chapter Eleven

"This is even larger than I remember," Joe stated.

He glanced around the crowd supporting all the vendors at the local farmers market. Ada had been thrilled when Gram came home and told them that Sarah would love for Willow and Ada to help her with her goods. Joe had been surprised but happy for both girls. Ada needed that help with math, which Gram mentioned Erin had suggested they focus on today, and Willow certainly could use more social interaction with friendly people and positive role models. Joe could think of nobody better than Sarah Spencer to leave the girls with today. And of course he and Erin would be close by if the girls needed it.

"It has definitely grown over the years," Erin agreed.

They both stood behind the long tables stretched with a variety of canned jars and baked goods. Four Sisters was a staple at the farmers market and he wasn't surprised there was already a line forming when Sarah and the girls had finished setting up.

"Should we help them?" Joe asked.

Erin shook her head. "Nah. There's no rush here. People are used to waiting in lines and they just catch up on their chitchat. I'll pop back in once I check out the other vendors."

Joe slid his hands into his pockets and glanced around the park. This sunny Saturday morning couldn't be more perfect. The rays from the sun seem to be shining directly on Rosewood Valley and the people milling about were all smiles. Families strolled from vendor to vendor, ladies with bouquets of wildflowers moved about, and some kids were off on the swing sets waiting for their parents to finish. It seemed as if the whole town had turned out.

"Care if I walk with you?" he asked.

Erin jerked her attention from the girls to him and he didn't back down. They needed to talk—even if it wasn't about the kiss, they at least needed to get away from the buffer of their girls so they could remove this wedge of tension that had settled between them. She was still Ada's tutor and he'd be seeing her for the rest of the summer.

"Alright," she conceded slowly. "Let me just tell them we'll be back."

He exhaled the breath he'd been holding when she stepped over to her mother and the girls to let them know they'd be close by. He hadn't planned on asking her to tour the market with her, but he wasn't sorry he'd done so, either. He never liked confusion or tension. He always believed getting thoughts and feelings out in the open was the best policy.

Yes, they'd kissed. Things were awkward. They also were adults with a strong past and clearly still attracted to each other. They'd done nothing wrong, but he also had to tread lightly because the last thing he wanted to do was get hurt... or break her heart once again. This time around, they also had two young impressionable girls to think of. They couldn't afford to break their little hearts, either.

When Erin came back to him, they turned toward the aisle of vendor booths. She didn't say anything, so he didn't bother, either. Having her company was enough—for now.

"Did you know Gary from high school started his own coffee business?" she asked after a moment. "He doesn't have a storefront, but he sells his bags of coffee here. Whole bean or ground, and it's really delicious."

"I didn't know that."

Erin gestured to the right. "He's usually set up in the next row. The blond roast is my favorite."

"You never used to drink coffee," he replied.

"It's an acquired taste and one I came to love when I needed more caffeine to get me through college." She laughed. "I had to use a good deal of creamer at first, but then once I found good coffee, I just drink it black."

He smiled. How else had she changed in college, when he'd been miles and miles away?

"I never would have thought you'd go for straight-up coffee. I'm definitely going to have to get a bag."

They walked a bit farther and Erin stopped at one of the vendors with handmade jewelry. There were small racks filled earrings, another with bracelets, and another with necklaces. It was the bracelets that had caught Erin's attention. She stepped closer while he hung back. Her fingertip ran over a delicate gold chain, then the charm dangling from the middle. He moved in just a bit closer so he could see what had fascinated her.

The tiny charm appeared to be some type of locket. He hadn't seen that on a bracelet before, only on a necklace. But Erin wore the same necklace as her sisters. That special pitcher necklace Sarah Spencer had bought all of them when they'd been younger. He doubted she ever took that off or had ever replaced it.

Erin looked at the charm bracelet for a good bit before coming back to him and gesturing that they walk on.

"You didn't want that?" he asked after they'd moved a few paces away.

Erin smiled and waved at a vendor as they kept going, then glanced to him. "Oh, I look at that bracelet each time I'm here."

And never bought it? Why?

"How much is it?"

She shrugged and turned the corner to the next aisle. "No idea. I've never asked."

"Why not?" he asked.

"It won't matter," she murmured. "I have to save everything, especially now. Even before the job crisis, I had to watch my spending so I could foster. My car is on its last leg, or tire as the case may be, so purchasing anything frivolous isn't an option at this point."

Yet she'd bought Ada and Willow matching hats for riding. That big heart of hers couldn't be contained or kept a secret. As always, she'd put anyone else's needs ahead of her own wants.

"Sorry," she snickered. "I didn't mean to just unload about finances when all you asked was the price of a bracelet."

The urge to reach for her hand and reassure her she had nothing to apologize for was much too strong. He clenched his fists at his side and kept reminding himself they were in public and they still hadn't addressed the kiss. The last thing they needed was to add another layer of confusion and intimacy to the mix.

"Don't be sorry," he told her. "I have good listening skills. I'm not judging or repeating anything I hear, so feel free to vent if you need."

She glanced up at him. "You always were so easy to talk to. That was one of the things I missed most when you left."

His chest tightened with grief and remorse. Even though he'd left to fulfill his calling, he still had a thread of guilt tied to his heart. How could he not? He'd hurt the most precious person in his life. While the parting had been amicable, and Erin understood he had to follow God's calling, that hadn't lessened the pain for either of them. Not to mention that tension that seemed to follow them in the few days between the breakup and his departure. Being in town without seeing her constantly had been agonizing. And when he left town, he'd tortured himself one last time by driving by Four Sisters. He still didn't know why he'd done that, maybe for some final private goodbye. He couldn't deny that leaving had left a piece of his heart damaged, but seeing her again, kissing her again, had soothed him in a way he hadn't thought possible.

But he was still confused and worried about his time here and part of him still felt like that teen who had to make a life-altering decision.

Instead of leading the way toward the final aisle, Erin followed the little stone path toward the gazebo. It sat at a far end of the park, looking the same as it had when they'd been in high school. She climbed the steps and he went right along after her. When she took a seat on one of the benches that ran around the interior, he sat next to her.

She stared straight ahead at the crowd. Her green eyes seemed a little more dim now than earlier. He knew she was struggling with personal choices right now, and as much as he wanted to offer advice, he didn't have a place in her life to afford that luxury. If she asked, he would help any way he could, but until then, all he could do was listen.

"I love this town so much." She didn't look away from the market and the sunshine and her words came out almost as if she were talking to herself.

"I just pray Willow can stay here with me," she went on. "I know that's selfish, but if he completes his rehab and the state finds him fit to parent again, they will remove her. But I truly think she's better with me than her father."

"I have no doubt about that," he replied. "What's the story there? If you can share."

Erin blinked and looked to him. "Her mother is gone and her father is an addict. He's trying to get clean, but it's a cycle. I pray for him. Nobody wants to become an addict. They just get wrapped up in the wrong crowd or make one bad mistake that ruins their lives. And now Willow is suffering for it, too."

Joe eased closer and laid his hand over hers. He couldn't just ignore her pain and he would comfort anyone in this position.

"She's thriving with you," he said. "There's no court that will be in a rush to put her back in a place where her father isn't capable."

"No, but they do put so much emphasis on reuniting with biological parents. I just can't imagine he'd be ready for a long time."

Joe leaned in a little closer and squeezed her hand. "Then enjoy what you have now and the progress you're making. Don't let worries from your future steal the joy from now."

A corner of her mouth quirked as she nodded. "I know that in my head, but my heart is so afraid of getting hurt again."

"It's okay to be afraid," he assured her. Yet the words had speared him. He'd hurt her once. How many times had she been hurt since? "And I never meant to be part of the things that have hurt you. I'm sorry I had a hand in that."

She said nothing as she pulled her hand from beneath his and glanced back out to the thick crowd. He'd obviously caused more damage than he'd ever thought if she wanted to remain so closed off.

"I don't think now is the time or place to get into our past, the pain that we still carry or what transpired the other night." She blew out a breath and came to her feet. "I should get back to check on the girls. It's a beautiful day so let's just enjoy it."

She made her way out of the gazebo, leaving Joe to wonder what had just happened. She was obviously upset about all the balls up in the air with her fostering and her career. Having him here in town might be more of a heartache than she wanted to deal with, especially on top of everything else.

And he couldn't blame her for wanting to focus on the present-day realities instead of the past. He had his own realities to face and some very tough choices to make. Ada had mentioned more than once about going home. While he didn't want to cut short his visit with his Gram or Dottie, he might need to consider taking that new position with the education Ada needed. None of that had seemed like a bad offer and with the way things were going here, maybe he should save Erin before things got any worse.

He had to pray on this decision even more now. He couldn't just take the "easy" road, but the path God had laid out for him. Joe had to do what was best for everyone involved, and having that weight on his shoulders would only make him rely on his faith now more than ever.

"So you have a ten-dollar bill," Erin said. "And the jars came to six dollars. So just subtract six from ten. What do you get?"

Ada chewed on her bottom lip and looked at the bag of

cash. She set the ten-dollar bill on the table and started to count some ones.

"We're learning math," Erin told the customer.

"Good for her." The older man nodded in approval. "Too many youngins' don't know how to use cash."

"Remember what I said?" Erin asked Willow. "We're at six already so start counting your ones from there."

"Seven, eight, nine, ten." Ada ticked off the numbers as Erin pulled out each one-dollar bill.

"That right?" Ada asked.

"That'll do it," the elderly man said. "You're a pretty smart little girl."

Ada beamed. "Thank you. Miss Erin and my friend Willow are helping me."

Willow stood toward the other end of the table assisting a customer with Sarah, though the girls had been helping each other count change throughout the morning. Erin loved how these girls just took to this under her mother's wing. They reminded Erin of her and her sisters.

A pang of sadness swept over her as she realized a new generation would be coming up and learning all about Four Sisters, but that generation wouldn't be Ada and Willow. Ada would be going back to Africa and Willow would ultimately be with her father so long as he got clean and remained that way.

Jenn's daughter and new baby would be the next generation, for sure. Would Rachel or Violet have the next baby? Erin felt so far behind on everything. Marriage, having a baby and now even her career. What did she have going for her?

"Have a good day," Ada told the man, then called to the next customer, "I can help whoever is next."

Erin pulled herself from the pity party. That wasn't how

she had been raised. She should be counting each blessing—
like time spent with this cheerful little girl—and not focusing on what she didn't have. God wasn't in the business of
giving handouts. No. He gave what was best and sometimes
she just couldn't see into the future. But she knew everything happening now would all be for her benefit.

Instinctively she scanned the crowd for Joe. She didn't
know where he went after she'd left him at the gazebo,
though she knew it wouldn't be far. She hadn't meant to
dump on him like that and sound passive-aggressive when
she didn't want to talk about their past. Hashing that out at
the farmer's market just didn't seem like the smartest idea.

And, she'd admit, she needed to put space between them.
He'd been so kind and concerned, listening to her worries
about Willow. The truth was he wasn't that person in her
life anymore. The one she worked out her problems with.
It wasn't fair to put him in that position now and it couldn't
lead anywhere good.

"How adorable is this?"

Erin glanced over at the customer in front of her mother
and Willow and couldn't help but smile.

Gram stood there in a Sunday hat with her handbag on
her arm.

"Garnet, what are you doing waiting in line?" Sarah
scolded. "You know I'd deliver anything at all to your front
door."

Joe's Gram just laughed. "Oh, I love getting out to the
market and when I glanced over and saw these two cuties,
I had to pop over."

"I've been working and making change," Ada piped up
proudly. "It's math, so I'm learning, too."

Gram gasped. "Well, you have been very busy and very
smart, too, it sounds like."

Ada simply smiled, so pleased with herself, as she should be. She'd been getting quicker and quicker with counting out bills.

"And how have you been doing?" Gram asked Willow.

Willow tipped her head to the side and shrugged.

"She's been amazing," Sarah stated, resting her hands on Willow's slender shoulders. "I think I found myself some new employees."

"You couldn't find any cuter," Gram replied. "Now, girls, which jams do I want for the church picnic next weekend? Do you have a favorite?"

"Strawberry," Ada exclaimed.

"Peach," Willow added softly.

"Then I'll take those two." Gram opened her pocketbook and pulled out her wallet. "I might as well go ahead and take that last blackberry pie, too. I can't turn down Sarah's fresh pies."

Erin worked at getting everything boxed up.

"Is Dad coming back soon?" Ada turned to ask.

Erin carefully placed a sticker over the pie box to close it and nodded. "I'm sure he is. He was shopping."

Ada laughed. "He doesn't like to shop. And when we do, he has me pick out everything. I hope he can do it on his own."

"I actually saw him buying coffee just a few moments ago," Gram stated.

So he had stopped in to see Gary. Good. Erin made a mental note to do the same before they packed up for the day.

Erin slid the box across the table as Ada took the cash and looked in the money case. Erin let the little girl work the math in her head and waited to see how she did.

"I think she gets six dollars back." Ada glanced over her shoulder to Erin. "Is that right?"

"Yes," Willow spoke up. "Good job."

The fact Willow offered encouragement to her new friend and was speaking more made Erin's heart soar. This was exactly what she'd wanted, and having Ada around helped Willow's social meter and her confidence more and more every time the girls were together.

But what would happen when Joe and Ada left? Because if the girls got too close, Erin wouldn't be nursing her own broken heart, she'd be consoling Willow as well.

Chapter Twelve

The doorbell chime echoed through Gram's cottage and Joe glanced up from emails on his laptop at the small desk in the corner of his guest bedroom. They'd been home from the market only a short time and he'd wanted to touch base with some friends back in Senegal while Gram, Dottie, and Ada prepared a lunch, which had been Ada's idea.

"I'll get it," Ada yelled through the house.

He couldn't help but laugh. As much as she missed her friends and her life back in Africa, she had truly adapted well here and seemed happy.

Joe listened as her footsteps pounded from the kitchen to the living room. As soon as his daughter opened the door, Joe instantly recognized the voice of their visitor—Pastor Matthew. He eased his chair back, closed his laptop, and headed down the hallway.

"Afternoon," Joe greeted as he stepped into the living room.

The pastor had already come in and Ada closed the door behind him.

"Are you here for lunch?" Ada asked. "We're making Daddy's favorite. It's a Robin or something."

Joe laughed. "Reuben," he corrected. "Best sandwich in the world."

Matthew also chuckled at the slipup. "That sounds delicious but I promised my wife I'd take her out to her favorite restaurant this afternoon for her birthday."

"Well, tell her happy birthday," Ada stated a second before she raced back to the kitchen.

Matthew shook his head and sighed. "That one is a bundle of energy."

"I'm aware." Joe laughed. "Keeps me on my toes for sure. So, what's up?"

Matthew glanced toward the kitchen entrance. "Can we speak in private?"

Joe nodded and gestured toward the front door. "Let's head outside."

They both stepped onto the porch and Joe shut the door behind him.

"Is everything all right?" he asked.

Matthew propped his hands on his hips. "That depends on you, honestly."

Now Joe's interest was piqued. "I'm listening."

"At the risk of damaging my pride even more, I have to admit my office and cell have been inundated with visits and calls about how much your sermon resonated with people."

Joe had also been approached more times than he could count since Sunday. Which was so nice since his sole purpose was to make an impact on the world and spread the Word. Yet he also didn't want to step on the toes of the man who'd helped shape him into the missionary he was today.

"I'm glad I could touch them," Joe replied.

"I wonder if all the buzz around your guest appearance made you think more about the offer?"

As if Joe could think of anything else. He'd weighed his decisions and still didn't have a clear picture. His prayers were still going up and he knew he just had to be patient and wait. That was the hard part.

"Honestly, it felt good to preach in my hometown and in the church where I grew up," Joe replied. "I didn't realize the impact I would have on myself, let alone the town."

Pastor Matthew nodded. "That's how God works."

Yes, it was. If only Joe knew if this was the right place. His stumbling block was Erin, if he were being honest with himself. She'd come to mean more to him than he thought she would. Ignoring this pull toward each other wouldn't be fair to either of them.

She wasn't the only factor, but since he'd returned they'd tiptoed around their past, shared a kiss and he'd upset her.

"If I can be frank…"

"Please do," Matthew replied.

"I want to combine both worlds." He shrugged. "I love the life I created in Africa and Ada doesn't know any other home. But coming back here has stirred something in me. Is my work done in Senegal? Do I start somewhere new?"

Matthew nodded and raked a hand over the back of his neck. "Those are all very valid questions and concerns. I wish I could answer them for you, but that's between you and God. Have you talked to Ada?"

"About staying?" Joe asked. "No. I haven't. She brings up going home and missing her friends. I don't want her to feel pressured or swayed one way or the other by trying to appease me."

"Understandable." Matthew rocked back on his heels and went on. "I also don't want to sway your decision, but you need all the facts. You needed to know how much the town fully embraced you. So much so, I'm afraid to get back behind the pulpit tomorrow."

Joe knew Matthew meant that as a joke, but there was a ring of truth to his words.

"But I want what's best for my church when I leave," he went on. "And I can truly say that nobody else even crossed my mind other than you. If you do decide to stay in town, we can make the transition as easy or slow as you'd like. I want this to work for not only us, but the church, and Ada."

There was so much to think about, and Joe couldn't ignore the ticking clock or the pressure that mounted with each passing day. How could both options sound perfect? He clearly couldn't split his time between two continents.

"Well, now that I've made you more anxious—" the pastor winked "— I'll head out."

Joe grinned. "Yeah, I appreciate that. And I promise, this is all I'm praying on. Well, for the most part. I'll give you an answer soon one way or another."

Matthew nodded, stepped off the porch, and headed to his car. Joe pulled in a deep breath and tried to wrap his mind around how much he was welcome here and if that was the sign he'd been waiting on.

The door behind him creaked open and Ada stood there with wide eyes.

"You're thinking of staying. Aren't you, Daddy?" she asked in a smaller voice than usual.

Joe merely pulled her in for an embrace because this was just one of those questions he couldn't answer right now.

"I'm not sure, honey," he replied honestly. "But I won't make any major decisions without talking to you. We're a team."

He didn't have a clue what was happening and that wasn't fair to her, so he better come up with something soon.

And it just hit him that this was the second time in his

life he was torn between staying and leaving while standing on this very porch and breaking someone's heart.

"Can you help me pick out some really cool things?"

Erin glanced in the rearview mirror and smiled at Willow. They were headed to find some door prizes and some decorations for the Back to School Bash. Granted they still had over a month to go, but these things took time and planning. Luckily for her, she still had her spreadsheet from the previous years that she'd spearheaded this event.

"Yes."

The little voice not only filled the car, but also Erin's heart. Willow was speaking a little more each day and Erin wasn't sure if that was because of Ada or that Willow had changed environments and felt safer now. Either way Erin was so thankful for the progress that had been made so far. Selfishly she hoped Willow could remain with her, but that would mean her father didn't get sober or the care he needed. Erin would never wish that on anyone. She prayed daily for Willow's father and wanted him to come out on the other side of this a whole new man.

As Erin pulled into the lot of the wholesale store, her cell rang. She tapped the screen on her dash and answered.

"Hello."

"Is this Miss Spencer?"

The unfamiliar voice filled the car.

"Yes, this is she."

"My name is Hannah McCormick and I'm the principal at Crest View Elementary School. How are you doing today?"

Erin's heart beat faster. This wasn't one of the schools she had applied to. She'd heard of Crest View, but it was well over an hour away from Rosewood Valley.

"I'm doing well," Erin replied. "And how are you?"

"Fine, thank you. The reason for my call is we have a mutual friend. Your principal is the brother-in-law to my cousin."

Erin shut her car off and dropped her hands to her lap. "It's a small world," she replied with a smile, hoping her joy came through, though she was still nervous for this unexpected call.

"I'm calling because we had a teacher go on maternity leave back in the spring and she has decided to take the next year off. I was informed of the budget cuts in your district and I'm hoping their loss is my gain because I've heard what a wonderful teacher you are."

"Thank you," Erin said, her interest rising as well as her anxiety over this next unknown chapter in her life.

"I'm not sure if you've found other employment yet," Hannah went on. "But I'd love to interview you if this is a position you're interested in. I know we're a good bit away from your town, but our pay is higher than what your district offers so I'm hoping that will offset some of the added travel expense."

Erin closed her eyes, trying to process this. Was this a sign she should be somewhere else? Did she live here and commute daily? That would take time away from being with Willow and Erin couldn't exactly take Willow with her or move, not under their current circumstances. Things would be different if Willow were adopted and not a foster, but that wasn't the case.

On the other hand, she hadn't heard from any of the other schools she had applied to. Granted it had only been a couple of weeks, but still, she couldn't discount an opportunity before giving it a solid chance.

"I would be interested in an interview," she found herself saying. "When were you thinking?"

Hannah mentioned a few date and time options and Erin settled on one at the beginning of the week. She needed some time to process and pray over this next step, no matter where she ended up.

Erin set up the interview and thanked Hannah before disconnecting the call. Twisting her fingers together in her lap, she let out a deep sigh. She truly wasn't sure what to do, but thankfully she didn't have to make that decision right now.

"Are we ready to go in?" She glanced in the mirror once again and found Willow staring out the window. "I have a big list if you want to mark off the items as we get them."

Willow turned her attention to Erin and nodded with a smile.

Before she could open her door, her cell rang again. She glanced at the screen, and when Beth Graham's name popped up, Erin opted to take the call on her cell and not over speaker.

"I'm going to step right out here, sweetie," Erin told Willow. "Give me just a minute."

Erin grabbed her phone and exited the car to take the call from the social worker. She swiped the screen as she hip-bumped her car door closed.

"Hello."

"Hi, Erin. Is this a good time?" Beth asked.

"Sure. What's up?"

Her heart kicked up once again. These back-to-back calls with so much uncertainty were not helping her already frazzled nerves.

"I want to be as transparent as possible with any information I receive regarding Willow," Beth said.

Erin leaned against the car as her knees grew weak. The

fact she had to preface the reason for her call did not sound positive or hopeful.

"I appreciate honesty," Erin replied, gripping her cell a bit tighter than necessary.

"Willow's father will be released from the rehab facility sooner than anticipated."

Erin closed her eyes and willed herself to focus on what Beth was saying. She couldn't fall apart now because having a meltdown wouldn't solve anything. She should be happy for him, and she truly was happy for anyone who was bettering themselves, but Erin was also human. She wasn't ready to let Willow go back and she worried how being removed from Erin's home would set the little girl back emotionally. Reunification was an important part of the system and in most cases worked for the best interest of the child. Erin didn't think that would be the case this time.

"Now, I don't know what that means exactly," Beth went on. "I'm not sure what will be decided or how soon. There's protocol to go through and he will have to be assessed and we will have to be confident without a doubt that she will be safe and secure with him."

Erin's throat clogged with tears. She had known this could be the end result, and fostering was about what was best for the child. She just hoped and prayed that Willow wasn't put back into a toxic environment or removed from Erin's care too soon.

"I understand," she finally replied. "Thank you for letting me know."

"I know this is hard," Beth went on. "Fostering is such a labor of love and many times hearts are broken. But you are doing the Lord's work and making such an impact with Willow. I hope you know that."

Erin nodded, even though nobody could see her. She

needed a moment to compose herself. She took a deep breath.

"I promise to let you know anything else I hear," Beth continued, "and I'll let you know when you can say something to Willow, but for now, let's keep this between us."

"Of course," Erin agreed. "Thank you for calling."

She disconnected and straightened. She didn't want to look upset or have any type of sadness when she opened the door for Willow. This was supposed to be a fun day and that was precisely what Erin would deliver.

Beth's words continued to echo in her mind, though. Erin was doing the Lord's work by loving and caring for Willow when nobody else could. At the end of the day, that was all that mattered…even if it cost Erin another broken heart.

Chapter Thirteen

"I don't know why we can't buy the giant blow-up jack-o'-lantern for Gram's yard."

Joe chuckled. "Because we won't be here at Halloween and I doubt Gram would want something so…large."

The word *tacky* had been on the tip of his tongue, but Ada clearly loved the ridiculous decoration. Why did stores put these things out so early, anyway? It was the middle of summer, not even fall yet. This wholesale store had it all and Ada had never seen a place like this. They didn't exactly have a store of this size or style in their town in Senegal. Any grocery items had to be shipped in and the costs were insane in comparison to the States.

"So we have to get a ten-pound bag of flour but you think the pumpkin is too big?" she asked, pointing to the twenty-foot blow-up display.

Joe shook his head. "Not happening. Gram sent us for her baking supplies so that's why we're here."

"I bet she'd like a surprise," Ada insisted.

"Then how about something like a pair of earrings?" he suggested, eyeing the jewelry counter in the distance.

Ada looked back up at the pumpkin that stretched insanely high. "I'm not sure. Earrings seem so boring. But this makes a statement."

This girl needed to become an attorney or someone in power. She didn't like taking no for an answer once she got something in her head. But he held his ground because there was absolutely no way this was coming home with them.

"Oh, honey, we don't need that."

Joe turned to the familiar voice and couldn't help but smile. Erin stood there looking up at the pumpkin as well and Willow had a wide grin and a twinkle in her eye.

"See?" Ada stated. "I'm not the only one who thinks this is cool."

Joe turned back to her. "Oh, I didn't say it wasn't cool. I said it wasn't going in Gram's yard."

Erin busted out laughing and he shifted his attention to the most beautiful sound.

"Sorry," she said between chuckles. "I just got a visual of Garnet coming out and seeing this."

Yeah, that was precisely what he feared.

"Can we?" Willow's soft voice never failed to surprise him. She was completely the opposite of Ada.

"That's not quite in our budget," Erin told her. "But I do agree the pumpkin's adorable."

Joe hated that Willow clearly wanted this and Erin seemed to be on board, but finances were an issue. He wanted to offer to get the lawn decoration, but at the same time this wasn't his place to step in.

"We're here for our Back to School Bash supplies," Erin stated. "And that will take up all the extra space in my car, anyway."

"Sounds like you have quite the list," Joe said, then had a thought. "Wait. Did you get your job back?"

Erin shook her head. "No, but I was asked to do the organizing since I'm the one who always has. I just couldn't say no. The kids and the community really love this."

Of course she wouldn't say no. Even at the expense of her happiness and mental health, Erin would want to put others ahead of herself. Nothing about her had changed, yet somehow she seemed even better than he remembered.

He certainly didn't need more reasons to find her appealing and adorable. He'd never met anyone like Erin since he'd left town and now that he was back, he wondered if anyone like her even existed in the world. She was so special...so perfect.

"That sounds fun," Ada chimed in, coming to stand near Willow. "Can I help you shop?"

"Of course," Erin replied.

Joe shook his head. "You don't have to do that."

Erin pulled a paper and pen from her purse and handed them to Willow. Then she pointed toward her shopping cart.

"Willow has the list and Ada can push the cart," Erin told him. "No problem at all."

Joe glanced at the trio of ladies staring back at him. An instant image of what his life could be if he stayed flashed in the front of his mind. This kept happening, like his thoughts were playing tricks on him or mocking him... he wasn't sure which. Regardless, he had a heaviness that settled uncomfortably in his chest. He knew God didn't make mistakes, but had Joe misread his calling? Could he have done mission work just as well here in his hometown?

"You can come with us," Ada offered. "We'll get done twice as fast."

Joe met Erin's gaze and she didn't look like she wanted to say no, plus he couldn't exactly leave Ada with her.

"That's fine," he agreed. "I can pay for Gram's flour when we all check out and we can use my cart for overflow. What are you getting, anyway?"

Willow held up the list and Ada tried to read it.

"Pen— Whatever that word is and chips. That one I definitely know."

"Pencils," Willow whispered.

"Oh, sorry." Ada shrugged. "Still working on that one."

"And you're doing great," Erin added. "Well, if we're all set here, let's get this shopping party started."

The girls went ahead and Erin remained behind them with Joe as he pushed his cart with only the flour. Yeah, this whole scene hit a little too close to home and seemed much more familial than he wanted.

He was sure Erin had the same thoughts.

"You didn't have to stay," she murmured. "I could've dropped Ada off at home."

"It's no trouble." He stopped when the girls spotted something on their list. "I don't really have any plans today and I think you distracted Ada from her pumpkin mission."

Erin smiled. "You never know, Garnet might just love that in her yard."

Joe snorted. "In the midst of her perfect flower beds? That's not very likely."

They went on to the end of the aisle and stopped again.

"I shouldn't be surprised that you're heading up this bash," he told her. "I hope they gave you money for all of this."

"Of course. And most of the stuff gets donated from businesses anyway, so the school isn't out that much. I mean, we can't afford to do everything, so the donations really come in handy for the kids."

He was still irked that she didn't have a job. When he went to say something, her eyes were shielded, almost sad. He wasn't sure what was on her mind and he also knew it wasn't his place to ask.

"Everything okay?"

Well, there went that pep talk he'd just given himself. Maybe she wanted to deal with her stress and worries on her own. Not that he thought that was the best way. Or perhaps she confided in her sisters. They'd always been so close, which was one of the things he'd sought comfort in after leaving years ago. He knew Erin would be surrounded by her loving family.

She blinked and sighed before smiling again his way. "Yeah."

He stared longer and she finally tipped her head. "Okay. No, it's not okay. But it will be."

Worry laced her voice, and he found himself wanting to comfort her yet again. But here they were in the middle of a large store with their girls just ahead. Now was not the time for him to wrap his arms around her or take her hand. He could lend an ear and offer support, though.

"What can I do to help?" he asked.

She tucked her hair behind her ear and pursed her lips. "Give me the answer I need for my next steps," she finally replied. "I'm just… I'm so torn with a new job opportunity that isn't ideal and hoping something else comes along. I mean, I haven't been given an official offer, but they seemed so interested that I have to be thinking of what I'll do. This is all new to me and I pray I make the right decision."

Well, they definitely had that in common. He wished he had the right answers himself. The pull from two directions, from two lives he'd established and loved, had him more confused than ever.

"And Willow's father is getting released from rehab sooner than expected and that honestly has me more worried than anything," she added.

Joe gripped the handle on the cart as that news sank in. He hadn't expected this and obviously she hadn't, either.

"Does Willow know anything?" he asked.

Erin shook her head. "I'm keeping it that way for now. She's making progress and I don't want to do anything to hinder that. When her social worker thinks it's a good idea, I will. I really do only want what's best for her."

"Of course you do," he stated. "I don't think anyone has ever doubted that."

"Can we get the colorful pencils or do they have to be these boring brown ones?" Ada asked.

Her question from the other end of the aisle had Joe and Erin redirecting their attention. Erin laughed and started heading that way.

"Let's compare the prices," she told them as she neared. "Colorful sound fun, but we need so many and we have a budget."

Joe remained behind them and listened as Erin carefully broke down the pricing and explained how to shop for a bargain. Her patience and soft tone was what made her so perfect for teaching. Being with children and wanting to help them clearly was her passion. He wondered what this job opportunity was that had her so conflicted, but he imagined her main concern right now was Willow's placement and well-being.

Once the pencil colors were decided, Erin put the boxes in the cart and came back to him. The girls went on ahead and rounded to the next aisle as Erin fell into step with him again.

"I worry when we hit the area with folders they'll be overwhelmed with all the colors and designs." Erin chuckled. "But at least we're out having fun and they're learning about math and helping our community at the same time."

"Do you always offer school supplies?"

Joe pushed his cart easily as he kept his eye on the girls. Willow would point to one thing and Ada to something else. He loved how Willow seemed to open up to Ada, talking more and being more expressive.

"The school fundraisers through the year go to aid in this part," she explained. "We have a business in the area that buys brand new backpacks for kids in need or any kid that would like one. Then I stuff them all with the main supplies: pencils, folders, notebooks. Some get crayons and glue for the younger kids. The older grades get binders to keep their folders in."

They continued on in silence for a moment before Erin placed her hand on his arm. "Look at them," she murmured. "The way they work together and get along so beautifully is amazing."

Joe nodded. "I've been watching. I can't tell if they act like best friends or sisters."

"I'd say both. I always got along so well with my sisters, for the most part. It's like these two have known each other their whole lives."

They certainly had a special bond and he couldn't deny they were both special girls, each with unique talents and attributes that complemented the other. Where one seemed to fall behind, the other would lift up. Children were the purest form of love and devotion. They opened their hearts so easily, ready to embrace others.

Erin's cell chimed from her shoulder bag. Joe kept pace with the girls while she pulled out her phone to check it. When she stopped in the aisle and seemed to be reading, he stopped as well.

"Everything okay?" he asked. Hopefully this wasn't more upsetting news regarding Willow.

She nodded and glanced back up. "Yes. My mother is inviting the four of us over for a movie night. She said Dad bought a new projector and is anxious to use it. Willow is growing more comfortable with the idea of going there and Dad being around so we're giving this a try."

"Good for you guys. That sounds amazing for all involved." Joe smiled as they started walking again. "I remember watching movies on the side of the barn with your old projector."

"Those are some of my favorite memories," she told him. "Growing up, we'd always have movie nights and Mom would have the best snacks."

"It was all those fresh cookies that did it for me," he replied.

Erin swatted his arm. "Or the company."

"Yes, of course. I enjoyed all my time with you...but those warm cookies..."

She laughed. "I guess I'll give you a pass. Nobody does cookies like my mother."

"And I've never had a better movie date than you," he replied. "We'd love to come."

Erin started to say something else, but the girls had another question about glue sticks. She left him to see what they needed and all he could think of was those summer nights he'd spent on the farm with the girl he loved. That girl was a woman now—a kind, carrying, generous woman—and despite what his head told him, he was getting closer and closer to her with each passing day.

"This is so cool!" Ada exclaimed. "I've never done anything like this before and I already know I love it."

Erin carried a bundle of blankets to drape over the square hay bales they'd be using as seats. All of this brought back so many memories, and she was thrilled Willow and Ada would get to experience one of her core childhood memories.

"You will definitely want to do this again before you leave," Erin told her.

Then she realized they'd be leaving next month. So soon. She felt like he and Ada had just arrived. What seemed like her world turning upside down when she first saw him had turned into something more than she ever could have imagined.

And she found herself wanting more from him than he could give. Once again she was back where she'd been years ago.

Summer was half over and the last thing Erin wanted to think about was Joe leaving yet again. Who knew when he'd be back? Would another ten years pass? Or would he come back sooner for a visit?

"Can we do something like this back home?" Ada asked Joe.

He had a jug of sweet tea in one hand and a stack of cups in the other. Ada and Willow each carried the snacks. Her father had set up a table for the snacks and he'd put out the bales earlier in the day. He was already behind the projector and as they got closer, Erin kept her eye on Willow to make sure she didn't get upset. But the way Erin had talked about her father to Willow and showed pictures and talked about the care he took with the farm animals, Erin really thought Willow's worries were alleviated.

"We don't have a barn or a projector," Joe replied, setting the jug and cups on the plastic-covered table.

"No horse, no outdoor movies," Ada grumbled.

Erin laughed and nodded toward the table for Willow.

"Just anywhere up there, sweetie. Then do you want to help me spread these blankets out?"

Her eyes darted behind Erin to where Will Spencer continued setting up the projector. He happened to glance up just at that time and caught Willow's attention. He smiled, then shifted his focus back to the task.

"You know I heard two little girls had the same favorite movie," he stated, not making eye contact with Willow again. "And I just so happen to have that one almost ready to go."

Ada squealed and jumped up and down. "Did you hear that, Willow? Now we can watch it together."

Willow nodded and gave the slightest smile, obviously still leery. That was okay. At least they didn't have to leave.

"Okay. Everything is all set," Erin's father declared as he straightened and adjusted those signature red suspenders. "Erin, you remember how to run these, right?"

"I sure do. Aren't you and Mom joining us?"

He stepped away from the projector setup and shook his head. "Your mother and I are going on a date. She says we never go out anymore, so I'm taking her into town to that new Mexican restaurant that opened."

Erin scoffed. "You've never liked tacos or refried beans in your life."

"No, but I love your mother and she works hard," he responded. "So if that's what she wants for dinner, then that's what we'll do."

Erin's heart melted. Both of her parents worked equally as hard and they both found ways to spoil each other, which was the most adorable thing she'd ever witnessed. That was the love she wanted. The kind where you gave it your all even when you weren't feeling it.

"Well, you two enjoy your night," she told him.

"You guys, too," her dad said. "Oh, and there's a couple of other movies I picked up just in case you want another or the girls change their minds."

"We won't," Ada called after him. "Thank you."

He waved a hand and smiled.

"Thanks," Willow murmured.

Erin wasn't sure if her father heard, but Erin couldn't be happier. Not only did they not have to leave, but Willow remembered her manners and this was a huge step in the right direction.

"You think your parents planned this on purpose?" Joe muttered next to her.

Erin jerked her attention over her shoulder and found Joe much too close. Not that she minded him getting near to her, but her heart and her attraction couldn't take much more to be honest. She turned and handed a blanket to Ada and another to Willow.

"Just cover all the hay, girls," she instructed. "It gets itchy without the blankets."

Once they were busy spreading out the throws, Erin looked back at Joe. "What do you mean?"

"This movie night with just the four of us and them leaving," he explained. "Sounds like a setup or like they think there's more between us. Maybe they've been talking to Gram."

Erin hadn't thought of that. She'd actually wondered if her parents decided to leave to make Willow comfortable and maybe it was a combination of that and what Joe suspected.

"Who knows with them," she answered honestly. "But I wouldn't put it past my mom to come up with playing cupid. With my sisters all married or engaged, I'm sure her eyes are set on me. Not long ago everyone was eyeing

Violet, but since she got engaged to Dax, I'm afraid their efforts have shifted."

Willow came back for another blanket and Erin handed over her last two. The girls bustled around making the seating area just perfect. With the glow from the projector, plus the twinkle lights that clearly her mother or father had put up since she'd been here last, there was ample lighting to see the expression on Joe's face. She couldn't quite tell if he wanted to say something about the possible setup or if he was staring again.

"Do you want to help the girls with snacks while I get the movie started?"

She had to remove herself from this intense situation. The last time she watched a movie like this was with him. They'd snuggled beneath a blanket on a cool fall evening. He'd always let her choose what they watched because he said he didn't care. And she honestly believed that. He'd always been laid back and put her first…until the day he hadn't.

"Sure."

He stared another minute and she thought he would say something else. Erin held her breath, wondering what he was thinking and if he'd share his thoughts. But he stepped around her and went toward the snack table, calling the girls over to get the goodies.

Erin closed her eyes and let out the breath she'd been holding. As she went to get the movie rolling, she couldn't help but wonder about the seating arrangement. Would Joe want to sit by her or would he try to keep his distance and keep the girls between them?

Either way this night was everything she'd always envisioned her life to be. For the next few hours she'd have to focus on the movie and not on this lost dream they'd stepped into.

Chapter Fourteen

This was a terrible idea. What had he been thinking agreeing to a movie at the farm? All he'd done was plop himself right into his past and he'd been trying so hard not to let those memories affect his future.

Yet all he could think, as the girls nestled between him and Erin, was how this could be their life. Each time they were all together, that was all that ran through his mind. He hadn't thought much of the life back in Senegal or his home and friends there. Ever since he'd stepped foot back into his hometown, he'd slid right back into that mindset of the man he was years ago.

Yet everything had changed for him. He'd left because of his calling for mission work, but he also hadn't been ready for that family life Erin had wanted. Being married and a father so young hadn't fit his goals at the time, and as much as he loved her, he couldn't put aside his goals to fulfill hers. She'd deserved someone who would give her the life she wanted. So while breaking both of their hearts had hurt, he'd had to think ahead and do what was best for the both of them.

But he'd become a father just a few short years after leaving, which had gone against what he'd envisioned for his life. God had had other plans. So what were the plans

God had in store for him now? He'd laid out everything so perfectly, as God always did. Yet there was something preventing him from fully committing to saying yes to staying here in Rosewood Valley. Was it fear of trying again with Erin and they realized they couldn't make a go of it? The girls would be devastated if they tried for a family together and then fell apart.

Ada shifted next to him and laid her head on his lap as the movie played. How ironic that both girls had the same favorite movie? Their similarities and personalities blended so well that he continued to be amazed.

Joe rested his hand on Ada's shoulder and glanced over to see Willow had also laid on Erin's lap. His eyes met Erin's and his heart clenched once again. Then she smiled. How many times had he seen her smile? Too many to count over the years, but this one...this smile caught his breath in his throat and left him without a thought. The only thing he wanted to do was close this gap between them and kiss her again.

Her gaze dropped to his mouth and he knew she had the exact same thought. Trying to ignore this new level of attraction with her was virtually impossible. And trying to figure out if staying in Rosewood Valley or going back to Senegal was a good idea also seemed impossible at this point.

If he listened to his heart, it told him to stay and see what could happen between him and Erin this second time around. But if he listened to his head, he'd hear that Ada's life and the new mission role he could step into was waiting for him. He'd wanted to start up his own mission for so long and had just been waiting for the right time. With Ada a little older now and willing to help, he could help grow her faith even more as he showed her how to be a leader as well. There were just so many possibilities in

Senegal if they returned and started this next chapter he'd been praying for.

"I think they're asleep," Erin whispered, still with that sweet smile.

Joe realized Ada's breathing had slowed and she'd stilled beneath his hand. He chuckled and nodded. "I think you're right."

"Do we just keep watching the movie and let them sleep?" she asked.

"Might as well, even though I've seen this one a hundred times."

Erin smoothed Willow's dark curls away from her face. "I haven't watched it yet with her, but I've seen it. I used to play this one at the end of the year for my class."

Joe didn't like that thread of sadness in her tone. He didn't know what this upcoming school year would look like for her, but he knew nothing would be the same since she wasn't returning to her old classroom.

"You'll have another class to play this for," he assured her.

Her eyes came back up to his and the sheen of unshed tears nearly destroyed him. He didn't even hesitate as he reached over and covered her hand with his. He gave a gentle, reassuring squeeze.

"This is a difficult season, that's all." Words he should take to heart himself. "You're going to learn from this and grow. You're going to be a stronger woman and teacher. This isn't the end of your career, only a mountain to climb and we both know God can move those, right?"

A soft smile flirted around her mouth and continued to torment him.

"You're right," she agreed. "I know that logically. I'm just scared I won't be able to provide for her."

"Everything will work out as it should." He found himself stroking his thumb across her delicate knuckles. "Worrying only steals the joy from this moment and your time with Willow."

Yeah, he was definitely preaching to himself. All this worry he'd bottled up with staying or going... It would all work out the way it should, but at what cost? Someone would be hurt or disappointed no matter the decision he made, but he wanted to do what God's will was. He just still wasn't too clear on what that was.

"I didn't mean for this fun night to turn into a counseling session," she joked.

"I love talking to you and if anything I say helps, then there's no need to be sorry."

Erin closed her eyes and a lone tear slid down her cheek. That innocent, vulnerable action broke his heart. He leaned slightly and swiped under her eye with the pad of his thumb. When she lifted her lids and met his gaze, there was something new in her stare. The sadness was still there, but a layer of...love?

Was that love staring back at him? Were they going down this path again?

Joe's heart skipped and the idea of fully loving this woman again and taking a second chance really started to take root. How could this even be possible? Both of their lives were unsteady and rocked with turmoil. Trying to rekindle anything now simply didn't make sense.

"You're still so easy to talk to," she murmured. "I've missed that more than you know."

She turned her hand over in his and continued to hold his gaze. He had to be honest and stop hiding from his emotions. If he was truly going to weigh all his options, he had to stop running from everything that scared him and threatened to question his faith. God was, and always would be, in control. Joe just had to remember to breathe and keep his trust where it had always been.

"I've missed our talks, too," he admitted. "And you."

She blew out a soft sigh and closed her eyes for a moment before looking at him once again. "This is more difficult than I thought it would be. I wanted to be upset with you or find that you'd changed and I couldn't stand you."

Joe wanted to laugh, but her words were so serious he didn't dare.

"And?" he prompted when she remained silent.

"You're the same," she admitted. "Exactly the same and having you here only makes me want what I know I can't have."

That bold admission took not only this moment, but his entire visit to another level of uncertainty. She could have kept her thoughts to herself, but she obviously trusted him in her vulnerable state, and to know he broke her heart and she still found comfort with him truly humbled him.

Before he could reply, Ada started stirring and sat up, causing him to ease back.

"Did I fall asleep?" she asked, rubbing her eyes.

"You both did," he told her.

Ada glanced at Willow, then back to the barn. "I missed my favorite part."

Joe pushed her wayward curls from her eyes and chuckled. "I'm sure we'll be watching this again soon."

"Can we do another barn movie night?" she asked. "I won't fall asleep next time."

Joe met Erin's gaze, silently asking her.

"I'm sure we can make that happen," she assured them with a soft smile.

And that's when Joe realized Erin was falling deeper

into this family setting...just like he was. Was a full family life in their future? And at what point could he make that final decision one way or another?

"This is the most beautiful day," Rachel stated. "I'm so glad we can all be here setting up. It's not often we're all together."

Erin handed one of the greenery garlands to Willow and pointed toward one of the round tables. "Just lay this on the table runner. It will drape down on both ends and that's okay."

Jenn and Paisley were bustling on the other side of the barn working on decorating food tables for the upcoming bridal shower here at Four Sisters. The farm-to-table event space had become so popular since Jenn came back into town and introduced this concept when the family was in a financial bind. Then Rachel had helped take over and now the entire family pitched in where and when they could whenever they were booked for an event.

It was still weird to see Jenn with a growing baby bump. Erin was so excited for her, Luke, and Paisley. Their little family was growing in such a beautiful way.

"I'm just glad I can join since it's rare I have a day off from the clinic or the shelter," Violet added. "But since I hired a couple newbies to my staff, my load is a lot less hectic."

"I'm sorry I couldn't come those couple days you texted me," Erin stated. "I've been busy in all different directions it seems like. The good news is I have an interview in a couple of days, but I'm not sure that's going to be the right fit for me."

"An interview?" Rachel jerked her attention from the

floral centerpiece she'd been arranging. "Why are we just now hearing about this?"

"I've been busy." She shrugged.

Working on the school bash, making new memories with Joe on the farm, holding hands with Joe…kissing Joe.

"Anyway, it's in Crest View so not the best option, but if that's who's looking for a teacher, then it's something I have to consider."

"It's definitely something to pray about," Violet added. "And maybe if you only did it for this year, something else would open for the next school year."

Erin nodded and glanced at Willow. "It's not just me I need to consider, though."

Rachel reached for another white bud and turned her attention to Erin. "You know any of us would help with her to make this easy on both of you."

"I'm sure she'd love to hang at the shelter and love on some puppies and kittens." Violet nudged Willow. "Isn't that right, sweetheart?"

Willow nodded and smiled. "I've never had a pet."

Erin sighed. No, she imagined Willow never had had an animal.

"I'll make sure we make a visit there soon," Erin promised.

Willow's face lit up. "Really?"

Erin nodded. "Absolutely."

"What are we discussing?" Jenn asked as she made her way over with Paisley.

"Erin's interview at Crest View," Rachel replied.

Jenn's brows shot up. "Crest View. That's—"

"We know," Rachel ground out. "That's why we're trying to be positive and help her out."

Jenn looked to Erin, then Willow. "Of course. Yes. Anything you need. I'm sure Paisley would love to hang with someone other than me or Luke."

"See?" Violet declared. "We've all got your back. Whatever you need, just ask."

The burn in her throat and nose was all the warning she had before she burst into tears. Erin covered her face in her hands as if she could hide her emotions.

"Paisley, can you take Willow and show her the horses?" Jenn asked.

"Hasn't she seen them?" Paisley replied.

"Show her again." Jenn's voice came out a little more stern this time.

Erin swiped at her face, completely embarrassed she couldn't hold it together, especially in front of Willow.

"I'm sorry," she murmured once the girls were gone. "I didn't mean to have a meltdown."

"Don't you dare apologize for being human," Rachel scolded. "Now have a seat and tell us what's going on. You don't have to be strong for us."

Violet pulled out a chair that hadn't been covered yet and pointed. Erin took a seat because there was no use arguing with any of them, let alone all three. Besides, they'd all had their own ups and downs recently. They were always there for each other no matter what. Erin just didn't like that it was her turn to need the attention and help.

"Is it the job?" Jenn asked, taking a seat next to her.

"Partially," Erin admitted.

"Is the other part Willow or Joe?" Violet chimed in, standing over Jenn's shoulder.

Erin glanced at her hands in her lap. "Yes. All of the above."

Rachel stepped up behind her and put her hand on Erin's

shoulder. "I was so worried when he came back. Then when I discovered you were tutoring Ada..."

"I thought I could handle my emotions, and I was, until he kissed me."

"What?"

"He kissed you?"

"I need to sit down for this one."

All her sisters spoke at once as Violet took a seat next to Jenn at the round table.

"Yeah, I didn't mean to let that slip," Erin admitted. "But there you have it. We kissed...twice...and we had movie night with the girls the other night at the barn and held hands."

"A movie at the barn? I didn't know we had a projector that still worked," Rachel stated.

Jenn rolled her eyes. "She said they've kissed and held hands and you're wondering where the projector came from?"

"Focus, ladies," Violet scolded. "We could have a second-chance romance happening and we need all hands on deck for this."

Erin laughed as she swiped new tears. "There's no new romance," she assured them. "He's not staying in town and I'm not going to Senegal."

"He's being considered as the new pastor," Rachel stated.

Erin jerked in her seat to look up at her sister. "What?"

Rachel pursed her lips. "I'm not one to gossip, but I can't help what I hear when I'm at the feedstore. Pastor Matthew is supposedly stepping down in the fall and Joe went and looked at the parsonage and that's one of the reasons he was a guest pastor."

Erin's head started to spin. He'd never mentioned any of

this. Did that mean he wasn't even considering it? Or was he considering but didn't want to say anything just yet?

She'd opened up to him the other night about her fears and concerns with her job, but he hadn't said a word. Did he not trust her like she did him?

"I take it this is all news to you?" Jenn asked softly, patting Erin's leg.

Erin shook her head. "I'm so confused about everything, but if he didn't tell me, then maybe I'm reading too much into that kiss and our evening with the girls the other night."

She wasn't sure about anything right now other than now more than ever she needed her family and her faith.

Chapter Fifteen

"I want to do something nice for Erin," Ada said.

With garden hoe in hand, Joe glanced up from his work on Gram's flower beds. She'd asked him to work on breaking up the dirt between the rows and the weeds. He needed the outlet anyway, so this was a win-win for both of them.

"What were you thinking?" he asked.

She took a bite from her cherry red Popsicle and shrugged. "I don't want you to think I'm silly."

Well, now she had his attention. Her mind was quite the fascinating place to be at times.

"I already think you're silly," he joked, resting his arm on the top of the handle. "So let me hear it."

She giggled like he assumed she would and muttered something around her Popsicle.

"What was that?" he asked, leaning forward a bit. "I didn't hear you. Don't be afraid. It's just me."

"Well, I was thinking how she's been helping me with schoolwork and stuff and then the horses and the movie night… What if we did something that showed her what our life is like back home?"

Home. Yes. They did have an actual home where the rest of their clothes were, with pictures on the wall, a church they'd made friends and memories with. To Ada, Rosewood Valley was just a fun vacation. To him... This town was definitely his past, but was there a chance this was also his future?

"So what did you have in mind?" he prompted.

"What if we cooked for them? Like dibi or thieboudienne?"

Joe thought of the ingredients in each dish and there wasn't anything he couldn't get here. "I like that idea. That's really sweet you thought of this for them."

Ada licked the melting Popsicle and seemed to hesitate.

"I also thought we could dress up," she murmured. "You know, like with the wax prints? I bet Willow would think that was cool."

No doubt, but how to get wax print skirts or dresses from Africa in a short time seemed like a stumbling block.

"I packed my favorite skirt," she quickly added. "And I have another one Willow could probably wear. I don't have anything that would fit Erin, though."

Joe wanted to laugh, but he could tell she was quite serious about this plan. His Ada had the sweetest heart and the most giving nature. Showing Erin and Willow a piece of their culture was actually a great idea, and Ada was right in that Erin had done so much for them. Granted he was paying her to tutor, but still.

"I think it's a great idea and don't worry about Erin's outfit," he assured Ada. "You and Willow can dress up and I'll just tell Erin to dress nice. How does that sound?"

Ada pursed her lips, took another bite and ultimately nodded. "I guess that will work. But we have to decorate and go all out. I want this to be like we're back home."

Another pang of guilt pierced his conscience. Ada clearly longed for her home all the while he'd been contemplating leaving the only place she'd ever known.

"You really miss home, don't you?" he asked.

"Yeah. I miss my friends and our church." She licked her sucker stick and went to sit on the little garden bench his Gram had for decoration. "I really miss riding my bike down the street. It's hard here because it's all farms and no sidewalks unless we're in town, but that's all businesses. Do kids not ride bikes here?"

"I hadn't thought about that before," he told her. "We ride horses and four-wheelers. But I bet you could ride a bike at the park. There are walking paths."

She nodded. "It's just different here," she added. "Not bad, just different. I'm glad I got to see it, though. Wait until I tell my friends I rode a horse and had a movie night in a barn! But, how soon can we do dinner? I want to make a few things for the table."

That little mind never stopped working and she'd always been so creative. He couldn't wait to see what she had in store for this party.

"We can also do something fun for the Grams before Gram Two goes back home in a few days," Ada suggested.

"They would love that," he agreed.

Dottie and Garnet had turned into the older version of Willow and Ada. They had just come together like siblings or best friends. They were at a church pottery class now with the ladies from Gram's small group. Everyone had welcomed Dottie like one of their own.

His cell vibrated in his pocket and he dropped the hoe onto the dirt and pulled the device from his jeans. One glance at the screen and his stomach knotted up.

"Honey, I need to take this call," he told her. "Give me one minute."

She nodded but remained in her seat, swinging her legs back and forth.

"Hey, Robert," he answered. "How's it going?"

He shifted slightly away from the warm afternoon sun as sweat trickled down the back of his neck. And the fact that his stomach had knotted knowing Robert was on the other end of the line was truly telling. Joe hadn't thought he was leaning one way or another, but now he knew. Going back to Africa for the next phase of his mission work suddenly took second place to a life here and a possible second chance with Erin. Yet he still had Ada to think of, and his little girl missed home.

"Going well," Robert replied. "How are things in the States?"

"Hot, but not like Senegal."

"It's pretty warm here today, I can tell ya that." Robert chuckled. "I won't keep you long, and I hate to keep pressing this matter, but the committee making decisions on the new mission startup came to me with another candidate they're considering. You're still their top choice, but they've moved the timeline for interviews up so they aren't keeping the other person in limbo."

Another candidate. That was unexpected. With the deadline shifted, Joe wasn't quite sure what to say here.

He glanced toward Ada who stared back at him smiling, legs still swinging. She'd just told him how she missed home and he had a call to technically decide now if he wanted to return.

He knew what his heart wanted, but just like the first time he'd left town, he couldn't simply listen to his heart and ignore logic and common sense...or his daughter.

"I understand," Joe finally replied. "So when do you need my final decision. Today?"

"No, no. I know this is a bit of a surprise so I requested

a week and they were okay with that. You are their first choice, so this decision lies directly in your hands."

A week. He had to make a life-changing decision in just seven days. Well, it would only be life-changing if he stayed here. Going home would mean getting back to his routine but also starting a new level of his mission work he'd been striving for.

He couldn't keep dragging his feet with this answer, but he was afraid to decide. Making a mistake wouldn't just impact his life, but his daughter's. His next steps could only be taken after prayer and patience and a clear conscience.

"Will you be able to decide by then?" Robert asked after a moment of silence.

"You'll have my answer before that," Joe assured his friend.

When Ada continued to stare at him, then offered the sweetest smile, he knew he'd do anything to make her life better and happy…even if that meant breaking his own heart all over again.

"Just wait right here."

Erin nodded at Joe as she stood on Garnet's porch. He'd extended an invite for a surprise, told her to dress up, and when she and Willow had arrived, Willow had been ushered inside, leaving Erin and Joe here.

She'd wanted to talk to him about the secret he seemed to be keeping regarding the position at the church. The fact he was contemplating staying gave that root of hope a healthy dose of water and sunshine. Yet the fact that she'd heard the supposed truth from her sister, who heard it through her business, truly hurt.

She'd have to wait, though. Both Ada and Joe seemed extremely excited for whatever this surprise was. Besides, they'd have to talk privately without the girls around, which would be a little more difficult since they were always around.

"Do I get to go inside?" Erin asked.

Joe nodded. "As soon as Willow is ready."

He slid his hands in his pockets and smiled and Erin couldn't help but get that giddy feeling all over again. He always did the simplest gestures that had her heart skipping a beat. Not to mention the fact he looked so handsome, but different. He had on a bright shirt with an interesting pattern in a variety of colors, his jeans, and a pair of slip-on shoes like a loafer. Very odd and nothing she'd seen him in before.

"And what is Willow getting ready for?"

He merely shrugged, clearly keeping another secret locked inside.

Erin tucked her hair behind her ears and glanced down to her yellow maxi dress. She'd been told to dress nice and this was her favorite dress that always made her feel confident and pretty. She'd left her hair down and put a little curl to the ends and even dabbed a pale pink gloss on her lips. She couldn't help but wonder if her efforts were in vain or if Joe thought she looked nice. Yes, he'd kissed her and held her hand and made her feel special, but he hadn't opened up. It was like that decade barrier wall remained in place and he kept himself emotionally distanced, and she couldn't help but feel that she was the only one being vulnerable. If so, anything she'd hoped would grow between them was impossible.

"Is Garnet in on this surprise?" Erin asked.

"She's aware of it, but her, Dottie, and some friends went to the church to decorate for the ladies' luncheon tomorrow so she's not here."

Before Erin could quiz him any further, the front door opened, and as Erin turned, she gasped.

"Oh, my word!" She exclaimed with her hand to her chest. "You two look absolutely beautiful."

Both girls had on the most vibrant skirts that went to the floor. They had on simple, plain T-shirts to match one of the many colors of the skirts.

"Come on in," Joe stated as he gestured to the open door.

Erin carefully stepped over the threshold and took in the cottage decor. The whole space had been draped with what looked like homemade flags colored in green, yellow, and red with a star in the middle. She had to assume this was the flag of Senegal.

Ada held her arms out wide and smiled. "Welcome to Senegal."

Erin placed her hands on Willow's shoulders. "This is so amazing. Did you do all of this yourself?"

"Me and Daddy," she stated with a proud nod of affirmation.

"And what's that delicious smell?" Erin asked.

"Just a little taste of home," Joe informed her. "We hope you like it."

"It has chicken," Ada murmured to Willow. "You said you like that, right?"

Willow nodded. "I love it."

"Right this way," Joe told them, pointing toward the dining room.

The moment Erin and Willow moved through the arched doorway, there were more flags draped from the ceiling making an X. The table had bright flowers and a wicker basket in the middle filled with napkins. There were name cards on the plates with French writing and their names.

"What does this say?" Erin asked Ada.

"It says *welcome* in our language. I wanted to teach you guys something since you've been teaching me."

Erin's breath caught as her eyes welled up. She glanced at Joe.

"This is the sweetest thing anyone has ever done for me," she told him.

"Me, too," Willow added. "Thank you."

Joe reached over and patted Willow's arm. "You are so very welcome. Now, who's hungry?"

"Wait, Dad," Ada interjected as she moved closer to tug on his arm. "Remember? The picture?"

"Oh, yeah." He nodded and laughed. "You know I'm not one for photos, but I did promise this one."

Erin couldn't help but laugh herself. "Oh, I'm well aware you don't like pictures. Our senior prom was proof of that. I have one photo from the whole night."

Joe shrugged. "It's not that I don't like them, I just don't think about it or care enough."

Ada rolled her eyes. "It's a good thing I'm in charge here."

Oh, there was no doubt in Erin's mind who called the shots with Joe. His sweet girl had him wrapped around her finger, but she had the biggest heart and truly was following in Joe's footsteps. They were both so giving and concerned for others and made the perfect team.

"I set the camera up over here." Ada pointed to the mantel over the fireplace. "You guys get in position and I'll set the timer."

"How should we stand?" Erin asked.

"You and Dad in the back and me and Willow will go in the front."

Ada went to the mantel and took the camera down as

Erin went to stand next to Joe. Willow came in front of her and Erin rested a hand on her shoulder.

Willow glanced up and smiled. "This is fun and I love my skirt."

"It is so much fun and you look adorable," Erin told her.

Erin's heart swelled with so much happiness and joy at seeing Willow having such a good time. This was the life she deserved. A life with no worries or fear of what negative impact would come her way next.

"Is everyone ready?" Ada glanced over her shoulder. "I'll set the timer for thirty seconds so I can get in position."

Erin nodded. "We're ready."

Just as Ada rushed back over to stand in front of Joe, Joe placed his hand around Erin's waist. Erin froze as the camera flashed. Had he meant to do that? Standing here like a family hit so close to home...too close. All she'd ever wanted was wrapped up in this moment and she had no clue where Joe's mind was at.

For now, though, she wasn't going to borrow trouble or worries. She would take this precious gift and enjoy the evening, then lock those memories with her others where Joe was concerned. She wasn't sure if she'd need to tap into those once he was gone. Her own emotions were all over the place so she'd shelve all of that for the sake of the happiness of these precious girls.

"I hope I didn't blink," Ada said as she went back to the camera on the phone.

She took it down and looked through the screen at the images. Willow went over to see as well, and Joe's hand fell from the dip in her waist. As much as she wanted to address that brief yet heart-pounding moment, now wasn't the time.

"What can I do to help in the kitchen?" she asked, pushing aside the questions she really wanted to ask.

"Nothing at all." Joe eased between her and the table and turned to face her fully. "You and Willow just have a seat and let Ada and me take care of the rest. I hope you like this dish. We worked hard on the menu for the evening."

She stared up into those vibrant eyes and tried not to get lost in them. As much as she'd tried to guard her heart, she'd only fallen deeper for this man during his short time back.

"I'm sure we will love it," she assured him.

He stared down at her a moment longer than necessary and she thought he might say something, anything that would give an indication as to where his thoughts were.

"We're having chicken yassa," Ada declared. "It's my favorite. It's normally really spicy, but Dad toned it down for you guys. I had thought of some other dishes, but I think you'd like this best. And I made *sombi* for dessert. It was my first time making it, but I think I did pretty good."

Could this moment get any more precious?

"I have no clue what either of those are, but it sounds like Willow and I are in for a real treat," Erin replied. "I can't believe you guys made all that and decorated so beautifully."

"The Grams helped with the decorating," Ada admitted. "But the food was all us. Right, Dad?"

She glanced at Joe with a look of such adoration. Erin didn't think she could love this duo more.

Oh, great. Love? She hadn't wanted that emotion to be so front and center, but she couldn't ignore how intense her feelings were.

Erin and Willow took their seats where their name tags were. The little round table with four chairs seemed so perfect for them. Joe dished up the main course while Ada went over a few basic words in French with Willow. Willow would repeat and Ada would offer encouragement.

"You catch on fast," Ada stated. "You're really smart."

Willow merely smiled and tipped her head, never comfortable with a compliment but deserving nonetheless.

"So are you," Willow told her.

"I have a best friend back home, but you could be my best friend here," Ada added. "Is that okay? Or do you have a best friend already."

Willow sat up a little straighter. "I don't have one."

Ada grinned. "So you'll be mine, then?"

Willow nodded and the two girls threw their arms around each other and hugged. Erin glanced to Joe only to see him staring at the scene before him. She thought she'd find a smile on his face, but he seemed...disturbed or bothered by something.

Again, she wished he'd open up to her. She wished he'd say something. Who did he talk to? His Gram? Ada? Pastor Matthew? Where did she fall on that list? Or did she even make the list?

So many questions and she'd have to find a time to ask him because with the way things had been going between them, she felt she deserved the answers.

Chapter Sixteen

"How did the dinner go last night?" Gram asked.

Joe cleared off the small table they'd eaten at the night before as Gram stood in the doorway. Erin was due this morning for a tutoring session and he still had the Senegalese decor up.

"It went even better than expected," he told her as he gathered the name cards and colorful place mats. "Erin and Willow loved the food and the effort. I really think we caught them off guard."

"I'm so pleased to hear that." Gram clasped her hands and smiled. "Is it too much to hope that you're staying in town? That you're maybe thinking of a second chance with Erin?"

Joe glanced toward the opening into the living room to see where Ada was.

"Oh, she's on the porch swing out front waiting on Willow," his Gram assured him. "I wouldn't bring anything like that up around her."

Joe stood up straight with his stack of place mats and sighed. "I'm not sure what's going on, to be honest. I'm torn which way I should go and I don't have just myself to think about this time around."

Gram stepped into the dining room and looked up at him

with bright eyes and a soft smile. She patted his cheek like she always used to do before giving solid advice.

"Have you asked Ada what she wants? Because she seems pretty happy here."

Joe shook his head. "I have not asked her. She's talked several times about home and things she wants to do when we get there."

"She might surprise you," Gram replied with one last pat before dropping her hand. "Don't discount her thoughts and make decisions before talking to her. If it's her future as well that worries you, then she needs to be part of the decision-making."

Why did this woman always make so much sense and put his thoughts on the right track?

"Or maybe you need to see where Erin is?" Gram added. "Have you two talked?"

"Not enough and the girls are always with us."

Gram took a step back and tipped her little chin a notch higher. "Then we'll fix that right up. I'll take the girls into town this morning and you and Erin can talk."

Joe opened his mouth but his petite Gram held up her hand. "No arguing. You have things to sort out and you can't do that by being stubborn or trying to figure things out on your own. Communication is key to any relationship. The relationship between a man and a woman or the one you have with God."

Again, she made so much sense and he knew all of this, but he hadn't known this decision would be so difficult. In his defense, he hadn't even known this "decision" would be an issue when he came to town. He'd just been coming for a very long overdue visit and for his Gram and Ada to finally meet in person—and for the chance for Ada to meet Dottie.

"Oh, and before you arrived, I'd never told anyone about

Ada," Gram added. "I didn't want word to get back to Erin and hurt her more."

Joe hadn't thought of that, but his Gram had always loved Erin and it was no surprise she'd continued to protect her heart no matter the wedge between them.

Before he could process any further, the front door burst open at the same time Ada's shout echoed through the cottage.

"They're here!"

Her excitement for Erin and Willow never diminished and Joe realized he'd have to talk to her before he made any promises or commitments to Erin.

"I'll give you and Erin an hour or so to chat," Gram murmured with a wink. "I'll take them for ice cream."

"Gram, it's ten o'clock in the morning."

She shrugged. "It's breakfast dessert."

Joe scoffed. "You never let me have breakfast dessert…"
She laughed and left him shaking his head as she went to the living room. He heard a murmur of voices, then squeals of delight from two little girls. His heart beat faster as he realized he and Erin would be alone to discuss the difficult topics. He didn't know what to say or how to begin just yet because he needed to know where Ada's thoughts were.

He remained in the dining room when Erin stepped into the doorway. She had on jeans and a simple blue sleeveless top with her hair in a ponytail and white sneakers on. There wasn't a time he ever recalled that she didn't take his breath away. No matter how she looked, her hair up or down, makeup or natural, she was the most beautiful woman he'd ever met.

"Is Garnet setting us up for something?" she asked, tipping her head and raising her brows.

Joe realized he was still holding everything and turned to set it all back on the table.

"She thinks we need to talk without the girls listening so she's taking them for breakfast dessert."

Erin laughed. "Breakfast dessert? I like that."

He turned back to face her and realized he didn't know what he wanted to say or where he'd even start if he did.

"You look terrified," she finally stated, her smile now gone.

Joe raked a hand through his hair and nodded. "I'm not sure how to do this."

Erin crossed her arms. "Do what exactly? Tell me that you've been discussing taking the place of Pastor Matthew? Or is that supposed to still be a secret?"

He jerked slightly. "How did you know?"

"Rachel overheard it at the feedstore and she mentioned to me thinking I already knew."

Erin turned and paced back to the living room and he followed. He didn't miss the pain in her voice and he hated that he'd caused her heartache.

"I'm surprised you never mentioned it, since we've talked about my job predicament," she added as she stared out the large picture window. "And I don't know why that bothers me so much when we never made promises to each other and you have no ties to this town or to me."

Now she did turn to face him. "I guess I just thought we were starting to grow closer and if there was something that important in your life, you'd want to tell me."

He took a step forward. "Erin—"

"No." She held her hands up to keep him at a distance. "I'm not trying to be passive-aggressive or have a pity party. I was confused, but then I realized maybe I was reading too much into that kiss and the way you held my hand."

No. She wasn't reading too much into those things. He just didn't know how to put all his thoughts and emotions into actions without confusing her even more. "I'm not sure how anyone found out about me considering the position of pastor here," he started. "And I wished you'd come to me sooner."

She shrugged. "I only found out a couple days ago and I thought if you wanted me to know, you would've told me. Then I thought I should talk to you, but we had the dinner last night and that certainly wasn't the time or the place."

"It's not that I didn't want to tell you," he said. "I was blindsided by the request, and staying here never crossed my mind until I got the offer."

Her lips thinned slightly. "I see. Well. It sounds like you've made your decision."

Now he did step forward, close enough to see that pain in her eyes and it ripped his heart in two.

"No. I haven't," he insisted. "That's what is driving me crazy. I didn't expect this job opportunity and I certainly didn't expect these intense feelings once I saw you again, but those are things I simply can't ignore."

Her eyes never wavered from his. "So what are you saying?"

Joe reached for her, curling his fingers around her shoulders and stepping closer. He dropped his forehead to hers and whispered, "I'm saying you're confusing me and I don't like the idea of walking away from you again."

He feathered his lips gently to hers as her hands came up to rest on his chest. Her simple touch and the way she seemed to melt into him had him ignoring all thoughts or responsibilities. All he wanted was to hold Erin, to spend more time with her, to find out what they could do to make this second chance work.

But he couldn't tell her that. He had no idea how Ada felt and he'd be selfish making a decision for both of them and blindsiding her.

Joe eased back slightly and framed her face between his hands.

"No matter what is happening between us, that doesn't mean I can make promises to stay," he warned. "I can't just uproot Ada from the only life she's ever known."

Erin pulled in a shaky breath and took a step back, forcing his hands to fall away from her. "You don't have to explain yourself to me. I know I was frustrated, but you're right. You have to put Ada and what you think would be best for you both first."

He shoved his hands in his pockets in an attempt to keep from reaching for her again. Before he could say anything, she sighed and went on.

"We've come full circle," she muttered. "This is just like before when obligation had to override anything we had. I get it. I do. But that doesn't make this any easier."

"I didn't say I was going back for certain," he reminded her.

The saddest smile came over her. "You didn't say you were staying for certain, either. So no more kisses, no hand-holding, or anything. From here on out until you leave or decide to stay, I'm only Ada's tutor."

As if an invisible wall went up between them, Erin had just put their relationship in a box and sat it up on a shelf. Maybe they'd revisit later, but maybe they wouldn't.

And just like before, the answer lay with him.

"Like this?" Willow held up a little bundle of suckers that she'd tied a colorful ribbon around the stick.

Erin nodded in approval. "That's perfect."

She'd had an idea to have some of her more mature students run a game stand and prizes were going to be simple like sucker bouquets, mystery candy bags, and a few passes to the dunking booth where one very lucky teacher would be at the mercy of anyone with a strong arm.

"Just make as many as you can, but if you get tired, then take a break. We still have a few weeks so there's plenty of time for these little touches," Erin told her.

Erin went back to the poster board she had laid out on the hardwood floor in her living room. She was making signs for each of the stations, which was much cheaper than buying them. She took her pencil over the plain board and sketched out some words, but her mind was still on the talk she'd had with Joe two days ago and the interview she'd had yesterday. There was too much uncertainty in her life between the job, the fostering, and the man. If just one of those three could get settled, she might not feel so overwhelmed.

But working on the bash details with Willow did bring some comfort because at least this was relaxing. Organizing this fundraiser was something in her life she could somewhat control.

"You look sad." Willow's tiny voice pulled Erin from her negative thoughts.

"Do I?" Erin asked, glancing up to where Willow sat on a pillow at the coffee table working on the candy bouquets.

"Are you upset with me?"

"What? No." Erin dropped her pencil and straightened. "How could I ever be upset with you? You're the bright spot of all my days and I love that you're such a great helper."

Willow continued to stare for a minute before going back to her project. The last thing Erin wanted was for Willow to ever think she'd done anything wrong here. Erin would have to do a better job of hiding her emotions or at least being honest so Willow knew it was okay to have raw feelings and discuss them.

The chime of the doorbell echoed in the tiny space, and Willow jerked her attention toward the door. Erin's first thought was that it was one of her sisters, but they would have texted. Was it Beth? Did she have news that could only be delivered in person?

Erin hopped up from the floor and hoped whoever the unexpected visitor was enjoyed her messy bun and sweatpants as well as the old ratty T-shirt she'd slept in last night. She and Willow were having a lazy yet productive day around the house.

When she peeped out the sidelight, Erin stilled.

"Who is it?" Willow asked.

Erin tossed a glance over her shoulder and smiled. "Your bestie and her dad."

Willow's entire face lit up as she came to her feet.

Erin thought about messing with her hair, but why bother? This was her on her days off.

She flicked the lock and opened the door wide. "Good morning," she greeted. "What are you two doing out today?"

"We came to see you," Ada told her. "And Willow. Daddy said he has to talk to you and it couldn't wait."

Erin's eyes darted from Ada to Joe and he only shrugged, which gave no indication of what this visit was for. As if her nerves needed another reason to be more...nerve-y.

"Well, come on in," she told them, stepping aside. "Do you guys want anything to drink or a snack? I made French toast for breakfast if you—"

"Erin." Joe's voice and that one word silenced her. "It's okay," he told her. "We didn't come so you would host anything. We're here on a very important mission."

"That's right." Ada nodded in agreement.

Willow came to stand closer to her friend and the two shared a smile.

"Well, I can't wait to hear about this mission you two are on." Erin gestured toward the old floral sofa. "Do you want to have a seat?"

"I'd rather stand," he told her. "You see, we brought you a gift and I'm going to let Ada give this to you and then we'll discuss our visit."

Confused and intrigued at the same time, Erin watched as Joe pulled a small velvety pouch from his pocket. He handed it to Ada and Erin didn't think she'd ever seen the girl smile so wide.

"Here you go," Ada told her. "It's from us, but I bet you're going to love it."

"Well, I'm sure I will."

Erin took the little pouch and slid her finger between the strings to pry the opening apart. Her hands shook slightly at this unexpected gift. She had no clue what it could be and she was quite surprised they'd thought to get her something. She turned the pouch upside down and shook the contents out into her hand. The moment the item was on display in her palm, Erin's breath caught.

"It's the bracelet that you were eyeing," he reminded her.

"You didn't have to get me a bracelet," she told him. "You already made us dinner and there's nothing I need."

"You might not need it, but I wanted you to have it," he told her.

Ada started jumping up and down. "Open up the locket."

Fascinated and curious, Erin slid her fingernail in the tiny gap and popped the oval locket open. A little image of their dinner photo nestled inside perfectly. She could've cried right there without another thought, but she held herself together.

"This is one of the best gifts I've ever received," she told Ada.

As much as she loved it, the gesture hurt as well. They weren't a family, would likely never be when Joe was in such limbo with where he wanted to be.

"There's more," Ada added, then looked at Joe. "Tell her what we discussed."

Erin shifted her attention from the bracelet to Joe and he had a sneaky grin on his face like he was holding the best-kept secret.

"You're looking at the new pastor in Rosewood Valley."

Erin froze, sure she'd heard him wrong. "What?"

"We're staying!" Ada declared, then looked to Willow. "That means we can be besties even more now."

Willow threw her little arms around Ada and they did some cute little dance that had Erin laughing, then looking back at Joe.

"You're staying for good?" she asked, wanting to make sure. She wanted to get her hopes up, and it was impossible not to after all that had already happened in the last few minutes. She loved both of them and wanted to hold them close forever.

He nodded. "Ada and I talked. We both love our lives in Senegal, but she has fallen in love with everything about this place and the people. She only asked to go back and visit her friends every now and then and to do video calls… but I think the idea of having a horse is what sealed the deal for her."

"Maybe," Ada laughed. "But I love you guys and would miss you too much."

"And I love you, too," Joe stated gazing at Erin. He

stepped forward, took the bracelet from her hand and carefully clasped it around her wrist. "I know it's not a ring, but we'll get one, assuming you'll give me that second chance and marry me."

Well, that did it. There was no way she could hold back tears now. She looked at Joe and just nodded her head because the single word *yes* wasn't coming.

He wrapped her in his strong embrace and pulled her close.

"And if you don't want to take that job in Crest View, we will work things out. I have savings that will help until you find something closer."

Erin didn't think her heart could swell anymore, but it did. His offer to lighten the burden until she found something that made her happy was such a Joe move and she shouldn't have been one bit surprised.

"Does this mean me and Willow are besties and we'll be sisters?" Ada asked.

Erin laughed against Joe's chest.

"That's what this means," he stated. "A family just like our first picture all together."

When Erin eased back, she looked to the girls and noted Willow's eyes had welled up with tears.

"Honey?"

"This is my dream," she murmured. "A sister and a mom and dad that aren't fighting and love me."

God might have closed doors in Erin's past that seemed hurtful at the time, but He'd opened every single one to get her to this point. Erin wasn't sure when she could adopt Willow, but until that hopeful day came, Erin vowed to be everything Willow needed to continue her journey through a happy, healthy and positive childhood. If Willow wanted, Erin would be a friend and mentor to her for life.

"So if we're staying and going to be a family," Ada started. "Does this mean we can go get that giant blow-up pumpkin for when Halloween comes around?"

Joe groaned. "I was hoping you forgot about that."

"Nope," Ada assured him. "And my bestie sister would like it, too, please."

Erin glanced to Joe and shrugged. "A horse and a blow-up pumpkin. Might as well jump into this family scenario with two feet."

Joe held her tighter and kissed her forehead. "I wouldn't have it any other way."

* * * * *

If you enjoyed Erin and Joe's story,
Don't miss Violet's story
The Sheriff Next Door

And the other stories in the
Four Sisters Ranch series
by Julia Ruth!

Available now from Love Inspired!

And discover more at LoveInspired.com

Dear Reader,

I hope you enjoyed Erin's story! If you've been following along with the Four Sisters series, you recall Erin is the fourth sister. You've watched Jenn, Rachel and Violet get their happily-ever-afters. I hope you loved Erin's emotional reunion story with a couple of adorable little girls thrown into the mix!

Reunion stories are just so fun and Joe and Erin have been in my head for quite some time. Considering I married my high school sweetheart, and we just celebrated our twenty-fifth anniversary, I really wanted to dive into this story with my whole heart.

I'm so happy you came back for Erin and Joe and I hope you fell in love with this couple just as much as I did. No worries if you didn't read the first three books in the series! Erin is quite capable of standing on her own, but wouldn't it be fun to check in on those other sisters? Of course it would be!

Happy reading!
Julia

We hope you enjoyed
Reuniting with the Cowboy
by Julia Ruth!

Discover all the stories in the charming
Four Sisters Ranch miniseries,
starting with Jenn's story in
A Cowgirl's Homecoming

Read on for an excerpt of the first book
in this delightful Western series...

Chapter One

The ranch is in trouble.

Jenn Spencer couldn't get the text from her sister out of her head. For the past few months she'd been on the verge of coming home, but that terrifying statement gave her all the boost she needed. She hadn't spoken to her family in years, but now it was time to put the past behind them.

Jenn glanced around the old building she'd be renting during her time back home—both the salon on the ground level and the apartment above. Her new landlord was late, but that gave her a chance to check out her new space thanks to the back door code she'd been given in the rental agreement.

The place certainly needed a fresh start...maybe that was why she'd felt so drawn to this old building when she'd seen the listing online. There were cobwebs and dirty corners that needed cleaning up in her own life as well.

And that revelation was yet another reason she found herself back in Rosewood Valley. Northern California had always held a special place in her heart, but three years ago tragedy forced her out of town. Thoughts that couldn't plague her now...not if she wanted to move forward. While her late husband was always in her heart and on her mind,

Cole would want her to mend those tattered relationships and live her life to the fullest.

She needed to meet with her landlord before she could venture to the farm and take that monumental first step. She honestly had no clue how she'd be received, but she needed to know how she could help save the place and restore broken bonds.

One baby step at a time.

Pushing aside the past and vowing to look toward a positive future, Jenn propped the back door open and made a few trips bringing in storage totes. She figured she had to begin somewhere if she was going to get her new life started...no matter how temporary. If things didn't work out, she'd have to face the consequences of her actions and possibly move from her hometown for good.

The nice spring breeze and the warm sunshine drifted in from the back alley, already boosting her mood. After about five trips, Jenn checked the time on her cell and wondered what was keeping her landlord.

Just as she lifted a stack of shampoo capes from the tote, a soft clicking sound echoed from the back door. Jenn turned her attention to the little brown pup that cautiously pranced through, with his little toe nails clacking on the chipped tile flooring and his nose to the ground as if following a scent.

"Oh, buddy. You can't be in here."

She took one step toward the light brown pup with his unkempt curly hair hanging down in his eyes. The poor thing cowered at her voice and scurried beneath the shampoo bowl against the back wall. Before she could figure out what to do with this unexpected visitor, the front door opened with the most annoying jingle. That bell would have to go.

Jenn straightened and shifted her attention toward the entrance as a tall, broad man stepped over the threshold. Like any true gentleman, he removed his cowboy hat upon entering. That simple gesture only revealed the handsome face beneath the shield of the brim. With his free hand he held on to an adorable little girl wearing a cute purple dress and matching cowgirl boots.

But the girl's hair had a serious wad of gum on one side. Jenn cringed as a memory of her childhood with her three sisters flashed through her mind. Another time, another mess of gum, more reminiscing she couldn't have prepared for.

"Good morning," she greeted, realizing this was her first interaction since she'd been back in town. "I'm not open yet, but give me a few days."

More like a month, but she had to get started so she could build back her savings. She'd just have to work with the dated decor for now and prioritize her needs and wants. Needs would be utilities and groceries. Wants…well, there were too many to list. Paint and flooring would be a good place to start. Maybe some air fresheners and a vase with some cheery spring flowers.

"I'm Luke. Your landlord," the man said. "Sorry I'm late, but we have a hair emergency."

She hadn't expected her landlord to be so…attractive. Someone older, retired maybe, with thinning gray hair and a thick midsection had come to mind. Certainly not a thirty-something man that seemed to fit the mold of a proverbial Western cowboy.

"She said she wasn't open, Toot," the little girl whispered, staring up at her father.

Jenn chewed the inside of her cheek to keep from laughing. What did this little cutie just call her dad?

The man glanced at the girl, sighed, then turned his attention back to Jenn. "We have an emergency," he repeated. "She's getting birthday pictures taken later today and *somehow* there's gum stuck in her hair."

He gave her a side-eye, silently expressing his frustration at their current predicament. The muscle beneath his bearded jaw ticked.

"Oh, is that your puppy?"

The little girl broke free and started toward the back of the salon. A furry animal clearly trumped a gum fiasco.

"Honey, you can't just go after every animal you see," he stated. "You need to ask if you can pet her dog."

"That's not my dog," Jenn explained, shaking her head. "He wandered in right before you did."

Jenn had no clue how her morning had gone from wondering how to finally approach her family, meet her landlord and unload her boxes, to dealing with a stray dog and a wad of matted hair...not to mention the unexpected attraction to this stranger.

The girl poked her purple glasses up with her index finger then turned to Jenn.

"Can you get the gum out?" She picked up a thick chunk of hair beside her face and held it out for Jenn to see. "Toot bought me the cutest ribbon with purple flowers that matches my new cowgirl boots and I really want to be able to wear it for my pictures."

Clearly this sweet girl had a favorite color. Jenn's heart clenched as another memory flooded her mind. Her own matching bows and boots, the excitement of breaking in a new pair as she helped her father on the ranch. But the love for boots had faded these past three years and Jenn hadn't touched hers since she left Rosewood Valley.

They were forgotten...just like her dreams.

"Paisley, she's not open yet. We can find someone else." The guy came to stand next to his daughter as he offered Jenn a warm smile. "I will come back to make sure you're all settled once I get her hair taken care of. She has an appointment with a photographer in an hour. I'm not normally this scattered but...kids."

He took Paisley's hand once again and started to turn, but those bright blue eyes gripped at Jenn's heart and she couldn't let them walk away. Maybe she couldn't solve her own problems with a simple haircut, but she could brighten this little girl's day.

"I'll meet you at that chair up there." Jenn pointed toward the front of the salon. "Let me find where my sheers and booster seat are and we'll get you picture-perfect in no time."

Luke Bennett always counted his blessings when he could, and right now, the great gum debacle was getting fixed and he nearly wept with gratitude.

He knew nothing about raising a little girl, let alone a hair crisis. But his late brother had entrusted Luke enough to put him on the will. When Luke had agreed to be Paisley's guardian, he'd done so never imagining he'd actually have to step into that position.

As Jenn bustled around looking in one tote then another, Luke crossed to her and lowered his voice.

"If you don't have the time, I completely understand."

Her delicate hand stilled on one of the lids as her vibrant green eyes met his. The tips of her silky blond hair brushed against one shoulder and the pang of attraction startled him. She had a subtle, yet striking beauty. No makeup, her hair pulled up in a high ponytail...she looked just like her sisters. Yet there was something about this woman that intrigued him. Perhaps the underlying hint of pain he saw staring back at him or maybe the mystery involving her return, he wasn't sure. And no matter if he found her attractive or not, he didn't have the mental capacity to take on anything else in his life...not to mention he refused to risk his heart again.

Luke hadn't realized when he rented the building online that his new tenant would be Jenn Spencer—one of the girls the Four Sisters Ranch was named after. The very ranch he had his sights set on. He'd proposed something risky to Jenn's parents about acquiring their land, but he'd yet to get a reply. He wasn't backing down...not when he had too much on the line. Time was certainly of the essence for so many reasons.

"I remember being a little girl and getting excited for bows and boots," Jenn said.

A wide but sad smile flirted around her mouth, pulling him from his thoughts. Something haunted her. He could see the raw emotion in her eyes but couldn't get caught up in her troubles...not when he had a whole host of his own to combat.

"It's no problem as long as you all don't mind I'm not set up at all and this isn't normally how I work." She laughed. "I've only been here a half hour."

"Mind?" Luke shook his head. "You're saving the day if you can fix this. I have no clue what to do with a seven-year-old's hair, let alone one with a tangled mess."

"Well, we'll see what we're dealing with. Don't give me those accolades just yet." She dug further into the tote and pulled out a black pouch. "Here we go. Now we're all set."

Jenn's focus shifted to the dog still hunkered under the sink. "Any idea who he belongs to? There's no collar and he just walked in from the back as I was bringing some things in."

Luke tapped his thigh with his hat and looked to the pup who stared back with cautious eyes. He inched closer, not wanting to scare the poor thing. And a quick glance had him smiling.

"Your he is a she," Luke confirmed, then shrugged. "If you care."

Jenn laughed. "I hadn't even thought to look. I've always had male dogs growing up, so I just assumed."

"I've never seen her before. She looks like some type of a Spaniel mix. I can call a few people while you're fixing Paisley's hair."

She nodded. "I can't thank you enough," he added, relieved this nightmare might be fixed and they wouldn't have to cancel birthday pics.

Who knew being a single parent could be so difficult? Each day brought on a new adventure. Of course those "adventures" could be called disasters, but he preferred to try to stay somewhat positive. He still had a garbage disposal to work on because a doll head had gotten stuck in there. He didn't even want to know how that happened.

"No worries," she said. "And forgive me for asking, but what did Paisley call you?"

Luke laughed and shook his head. "Toot. It's a long story. I'm so used to it, I don't think about what other people wonder when they hear it."

"Sounds like a special relationship."

Jenn smiled once again before crossing the salon toward Paisley. *Special friendship* was a very mild way of putting things, considering he'd gone from long-distance uncle to permanent guardian in the proverbial blink of an eye.

Moving from Oregon to California and trying to start

a new life, a new business, and put all of Paisley's needs first while dealing with the grief of losing his brother and sister-in-law had been the hardest time of his life. Not to mention the rental agreement on his brother's home was up in two months. They'd been preparing to build so they'd just been renting a small cottage, which was where he and Paisley lived.

He honestly didn't know how people got through such tragic events without their faith. He'd gotten on his knees in prayer so many times, begging God to give him the guidance to take on the role of father and make the best decisions for this new life he and Paisley shared.

Luke pulled out his cell and sent out several messages, trying to shift his focus from his own problems and worries to the misplaced pup. Hopefully he'd hear something soon. He highly doubted Jenn had the time or the space to keep a dog considering she was new to town.

"You know, I got gum in my sister's hair when I was little?" Jenn said.

Luke turned his attention toward the pair. Paisley sat perfectly still in the salon chair with a black cape around her shoulders as Jenn seemed to be examining the damage.

"You did?" Paisley asked, her eyes wide with curiosity. "Was she mad?"

"She was at first until our mom took her to get a new haircut and she loved the new style so much, she thanked me for the accident. Now, my mom—that's a different story. I had to do dishes every night for a month."

Paisley smiled and a warmth spread over Luke's heart. Smiles had been few and far between as of late, and no matter how short the happiness, he'd take it. That's all he wanted for his niece. Yet a sliver of guilt hit him as he listened to Jenn speak of her family. The way her father had insisted on keeping the potential sale of the family ranch a secret had Luke convinced that there had to be under-lying friction with the homestead. He wasn't trying to rip the family apart, he just wanted a piece of their farm. He couldn't feel guilty for trying to provide the best life for Paisley.

A piece of land with a barn would be so ideal. He could renovate the large building for the livestock he tended to and he could build a nice, modest home for him and Pais-ley to start their lives. There was no secret in town that the Four Sisters Ranch had hit hardship. Wasn't this the best solution for everyone involved?

"I think if we cut just a little and make some layers around your face, we'll be good to go."

"Can I still wear my bow?" his niece asked, her eyes wide with worry.

"Absolutely." Jenn turned the chair away from the mir-ror. "I don't want you to see until I'm all done."

"Like a surprise?"

Jenn nodded. "This is definitely a surprise."

Luke kept his eye on the dog, who seemed to be perfectly content tucked in the corner. He'd been a veterinarian for five years now. While he specialized in larger farm animals, he'd learned early on that all God's creatures were essen-tially the same. They had true feelings, fears and instinct. This dog probably knew she was safe in here, but the pup still kept a watchful eye on them, just in case.

The girls chatted about hair and boots, and Luke real-ized how much Paisley needed female conversation. He made a mental note to add pampering into a monthly rou-tine for Sweet P. Coming to a salon and having someone do her hair, plus girl talk, was exactly what Paisley needed in her life right now. Would this make up for all she'd lost?

Absolutely not, but Luke planned on integrating positive moments every chance he could get.

Moving any female into his life on any level would be difficult. The scar left behind by his runaway fiancée still seemed too fresh, but he had to put that hurt in the very back of his mind because that chapter in his life paled in comparison to this current chapter.

He glanced back to the dog, who had finally fallen asleep. Likely someone in town was missing their family pet and hopefully they'd put a collar on her once she returned home.

"What do we think?"

Luke looked back just as Jenn spun the chair around for Paisley to see her reflection in the mirror. Jenn fluffed the blond hair around Paisley's shoulders and his niece's smile widened. His heart swelled with a happiness he'd been missing over the past few months.

"Do you like it?" Jenn asked.

"I look older." Paisley beamed. "I love it."

Jenn caught his eyes in the mirror. "Sorry about that," she said, cringing. "I wasn't going for older. I was going for gum-free."

Luke shook his head. "Gum-free was the goal," he agreed. "I think she looks beautiful."

"You have to say that," Paisley argued.

"Who says?" he countered.

Paisley pursed her little lips, thinking of a reply, when his cell vibrated in his pocket. He pulled it out and glanced at Jenn. Her striking eyes still held his and his heart beat a bit quicker. Good thing he had a call to pull his attention away from the beauty threatening to steal his focus.

"Hopefully this is someone about the dog," he explained

before he turned to take the call from a number he didn't recognize.

"This is Luke."

"Mr. Bennett, this is Helen Myers from Beacon Law Firm. Is this a good time?"

He glanced to the girls, who had eyes on him, wondering if he had news about the pup. He shook his head and covered the cell.

"I need to take this," he whispered as he moved to the back of the salon.

He had no idea why a law firm would be calling him, and this wasn't even the firm that had handled his brother's will.

"I'm sorry, what did you say this was about?" Luke asked as he got to the open back door.

"I didn't, but my client Carol Stephens is seeking guardianship for Paisley Bennett and I need to set up a time to meet with you and your attorney. She would like to make this as seamless as possible for the child."

A pleasant breeze blew in from the open back door, random noises from the alley out back seemed to echo off the buildings, and Paisley and Jenn had started chatting once again. But all he heard was that someone wanted guardianship of his niece. *His* niece.

"I don't even know who this Carol is," he stated, then rattled off his lawyer's name. "You can call her if you need any further information, but the will was clear on who Paisley would be with. The name Carol wasn't even in the documents so I doubt she has a strong connection to my brother."

"She didn't think her name would be in the will, but that's a long story and one of the many reasons we need a meeting. Carol was Talia's best friend and cousin. She's the only family member Talia has left, but she's been overseas in the military. She's home now and is seeking custody."

Luke's hat dropped from his hand. He leaned against the doorjamb and attempted to calm his breathing. Getting worried or worked up wouldn't help things and he had no idea if this call was even legit.

But he did know that he was the only family member left on this side and Talia apparently was the only family member left on the other. Was that what this would all come down to? A ball of dread settled hard in his stomach.

"I'm not saying another word," he informed the woman. "If you need anything, you can call my lawyer, but Paisley is going nowhere."

With that sickening weight in his gut, he disconnected the call. Nobody could take his niece from him...could they?

Chapter Two

"I need help."

Jenn clutched the dog in her arms and raced through the doors of the vet's office. The tiny waiting area with only three chairs was empty, but she'd seen a truck out front so she hoped someone was available. Fear consumed her as she glanced around for anyone to fix this problem.

"Hello?" she called.

"Jenn." Paisley jumped up from behind the receptionist desk and came around, her eyes wide. "What happened?"

Shaking, Jenn looked toward the doors that led to the back, hoping someone would come out. Any adult or provider who could take over this dire situation.

"I think she ate some of my hair color," she explained, swallowing the tears clogging her throat. "Is the vet here?"

"In the back. Come on."

Paisley led the way as she started calling out for Toot. Any other time she'd still find that name amusing, but right now her nerves were on edge and her heart beat much too fast.

Luke stepped into the narrow hallway from a side room, his eyes wide as he took in the sight. She'd had no idea he'd taken over Charles Major's clinic, but now wasn't the time for questions or trying to get to know her new landlord any better. She knew the old vet, as Charles had helped on her family's farm for years. But she wasn't going to get picky now.

"Jenn," Luke called.

He moved quickly, taking the dog from her. He led them into another room down the hallway. Luke lay the dog on the sterile metal table and turned his concerned eyes to her. Even in the midst of this chaos, an unexpected jolt of awareness hit her hard. She couldn't allow her thoughts to stray or become too distracted by a handsome stranger.

"What happened?" he asked in a voice much too calm in comparison to her own nerves.

She explained how she was in the front display windows using her vacuum for the dust and cobwebs when she heard commotion in the back and found the pup in the dispensary. Hair color covered the fur around her mouth and paws, tubes of color were all over the floor.

"Please tell me I didn't kill this poor dog!" she cried.

What a day for her first transition back into town. She hadn't even gotten the courage to go see the farm or her parents yet because she'd been procrastinating by cleaning and running over her speech in her head for when she finally landed on their doorstep.

What could she say to make up for all those years she'd stayed away? When she'd left Rosewood Valley after Cole suddenly passed, she'd been so angry and heartbroken. She'd said terrible things to her father, blamed him for Cole's death. She'd wanted her family out of her life…and now she needed to make amends.

"I'm not sure what's going on yet." Luke went into full work mode, his focus only on the dog now. "Let me do an assessment and run some tests. Why don't you go wait with Paisley in the lobby and I'll let you know something soon."

"I'll wait here."

He shot those piercing blue eyes over his shoulder, but

she held her ground and tipped her chin, silently daring him to make her leave.

In a flash, she recalled another time and place...another man. Cole used to get perturbed with her when she'd wanted to hang in the barns when animals were giving birth. He wanted space to work and didn't want her around if something bad happened. Always trying to shield and protect her from the messy bits of life.

Very likely that's why Luke wanted her gone now. But she wasn't going anywhere. Life was messy—there was no getting around that fact. She'd tried running from her past mess and now she had an even bigger one to clean up, so here she was back in her hometown and ready to tackle whatever she needed to set her life back on the right path.

Because she respected Luke and his position, she did step back to the corner to stay out of his way. Jenn marveled at the way he was so gentle yet efficient with the pup. Luke asked her a few questions as he worked and informed her he'd know more after the tests were run.

Just having his calm voice in her moment of panic really settled her nerves. As if his looks weren't enough of an attraction, now he had charm and comforting mannerisms...all qualities in her late husband that she both loved and missed.

She couldn't be attracted to her landlord. She didn't want that reminder of all she'd lost when her husband passed. A man with a child was everything she'd been hoping for, but that was another lifetime ago.

This phase in her life was all about a fresh start, repairing relationships with her family and saving her farm. Nothing more.

"Good news." Luke came back into the small exam room to find Jenn stroking the pup's tan fur. "Doesn't look like anything toxic in her bloodstream. I don't believe she ingested anything, but we will keep a close eye on her to make sure she's acting okay."

Jenn straightened and blew out a sigh. "That's a relief. I thought she was sleeping the whole time I was cleaning and I had no idea she'd gotten into anything. I'm not an irresponsible person—"

Luke gave her shoulder a reassuring squeeze. "It's okay. Accidents happen and I never thought you did anything on purpose."

A tender smile spread across her face. And as beautiful as she was, it was the red-rimmed eyes that tugged at his heart. She obviously had a soft spot for animals. She'd grown up on a farm and hadn't ejected the stray pup from her shop, and he was sure there was likely some code or rule against animals in that type of business.

Why did he have to find her so adorable in a way that completely surprised him? He'd seen her sisters around the farm and in town and not one of them, while each pretty in their own way, had even remotely ruffled his interest. He didn't have time to start a relationship and there were too many reasons he shouldn't.

The main one being he'd just found himself in a custody dispute and he still wanted a piece of the Four Sisters farmland. Was that why she'd come home? Did she know they were thinking of selling? What had Jenn heard?

He had no idea what brought her home, but he knew he still needed to keep quiet. None of this was his place to address. Whatever happened between him and Will and Sarah Spencer was between them. If they wanted to bring their girls in on the proposal, that was their business, but until he knew for sure what Jenn was aware of, Luke would remain true to his word.

Luke couldn't help but wonder why Jenn hadn't taken

the dog to her sister, Violet. Vi was the small-animal vet in town. Were the sisters not on speaking terms? Granted his office was closer to Jenn's salon, but still. Odd that she didn't go to family first.

There had to be a rift, but he shouldn't concern himself with anyone else's business. Not only did he have enough on his own plate, he'd been so burned before, the last thing he needed was to get swept away in someone else's woes.

"Can I take her home?" Jenn asked, breaking into his thoughts.

Luke stepped back. "Does that mean you're keeping her?"

Jenn reached up and tightened her ponytail as her eyes traveled back to the dog, who didn't seem to have a worry in the world.

"I can't just toss her out," she admitted. "I hope pets are allowed in the building you rented me."

Luke laughed. "Of all people, you think I'm going to say no to your pet?"

"She's not *my* pet," Jenn corrected, focusing back on him. "But I'll keep her until we can find a home."

Luke nodded. "Fair enough."

He went over instructions and what to watch for once they left. He also let her know he'd be stopping by just to check in. Maybe he could have her come to the clinic, but he didn't mind stopping at the shop to see her—

No. To see the dog. He had to get his head on straight and focus on what was important. Paisley and buying a portion of the farm, in that order. Nothing else mattered.

"Toot."

Luke turned toward the door where Paisley stood in the opening holding up a dog treat in the shape of a sugar cookie. One bite had been taken and Paisley's nose wrinkled in disgust. They'd had her birthday pictures just a few hours ago and he'd come into the clinic to work on inventory. Thankfully they were here when Jenn came with her emergency.

"These cookies are terrible," she told him. "Where did you get them?"

Luke raked a hand over his jaw. "Those are dog treats, Sweet P. They are just made to look like human cookies."

The little girl's nose wrinkled. "Oops. Sorry. They were at the counter so I thought they were for people."

Jenn snickered and he glanced over his shoulder, pleased to see a smile as opposed to the sheer terror he'd seen on her face when she'd arrived.

"It's always something," he muttered, shaking his head. "So don't feel too bad about the pup. Paisley's eating dog treats."

He truly didn't know how he could keep an eye on her, run a clinic, try to fight for custody and get land secured for their future. He wasn't giving up, but he wouldn't mind catching a break.

"Is Jenn's dog okay?" Paisley asked. "Can she have the rest of my cookie?"

"I think the dog will be just fine," Luke told her. "And, yes, she'd probably like the rest of the cookie."

"That's a good name for her, don't you think?" Paisley asked, looking to Jenn for an answer.

Jenn tipped her head and grinned. "Cookie. I think that's a perfect name."

As Luke watched the two ladies fawn over the dog and the treat, he couldn't help but see a life he once thought he would have. A wife, a child, definitely pets. But four years ago his fiancée decided that wasn't her vision at all and left him standing at the altar like some fool. He'd learned his lesson and hunkered down into his work from then on out… until now when his focus shifted from himself to his niece.

"What else do you own in this town?"

Jenn's question pulled him from his thoughts. "Excuse me?"

"My building, you're a vet… Anything else you own I should be aware of? I feel like I'm going to go get a gallon of milk and you'll be my checkout clerk."

Her quick wit had him chuckling. "No. This is all I do. You're safe to get your milk."

The building she was in had belonged to his late brother who had just purchased with intentions of renting. His family saga and tragedies weren't necessary to get into right now. She'd no doubt find out enough if she listened around town.

The cell in his pocket vibrated and he excused himself.

Will Spencer, Jenn's father.

"I need to take this," he told her, feeling a bit awkward as he did.

Luke stepped into the hall, hoping the man was calling with an agreement to sell or at least a counteroffer. He needed that stability now more than ever. A solid plan for the future would go a long, long way in proving that he was the only option for guardianship of his niece.

A Cowgirl's Homecoming
*and more titles by Julia Ruth
are available now from
Love Inspired!*

*And discover more at
LoveInspired.com*

Harlequin® Reader Service

Enjoyed your book?

Try the perfect subscription for Romance readers and get more great books like this delivered right to your door.

See why over 10+ million readers have tried Harlequin Reader Service.

Start with a Free Welcome Collection with free books and a gift—valued over $20.

Choose any series in print or ebook.
See website for details and order today:

TryReaderService.com/subscriptions